Hart of Country

I0677248

KRIS NACOLE

Dedication

Mom:

Thank you for always being there for me without hesitation, and thank you for pushing me along this journey by encouraging me to continue chasing my dreams. I couldn't have asked for a better role model in my life or nana for the boys. I love you to the moon.

Hart of Country is also dedicated to anyone who has ever lost themselves after losing a loved one. Sometimes it's hard to pick up the pieces and move forward, especially when you loved that person with your whole heart. Don't be afraid to open your heart again when you're ready, but remember there is no time limit when it comes to grieving. Take the time you need, and when the time is right, put one foot in front of the other and work toward finding yourself again. It's okay to fall in love and be happy. Everyone deserves love and happiness.

Prologue

Kailyn

Whitefish, MT

MY HEAD ACHED AND throbbed as I blinked my eyes open and struggled to focus on the bright flashing lights in the distance.

What's going on? Where am I?

The smell of burnt rubber and gasoline assaulted my lungs.

A deep voice bellowed through the darkness. "Miss. Miss, can you hear me?"

The constant ringing in my ears and the sirens blaring around me made it hard to hear him.

"Help is coming. Hang in there," the voice said again.

What happened?

Trying to remember, I groaned and winced as I touched my face.

Why does everything hurt so badly?

Blinking through blurred vision, I scanned the area. Blue and red lights flashed all around me, making me even more disoriented and confused. I was in a lot of pain, and I couldn't remember why. The last thing I remembered was leaving my friend Leesa's wedding reception with my boyfriend, Mason, to head back to our hotel.

A firefighter grunted as he yanked on the door. "Don't move. We're gonna get you out of there. Just be still and keep your eyes closed." He turned and grabbed a large piece of equipment from another man behind him. "This is going to be loud. I'm sorry."

The screeching of grinding steel tore through my pounding head and down my spine like nails against a chalkboard.

What is he doing? Am I dreaming?

As my vision cleared, silhouettes of people on the sidewalk, gawking in my direction, confused me even more.

I reached over to the driver's seat. "Mason?" I mumbled, barely able to speak. Mason had been driving. I did remember that. "Ouch." I jerked my hand back, my finger throbbing after grazing it against something sharp.

Glass? Shattered glass was scattered everywhere.

I tried turning my head to see if Mason was okay, but a sharp pain shot down my neck and between my shoulders.

"Ma'am, please stop moving until we can get you checked out. We're almost there." The firefighter chomped away at the metal with the large tool he was holding.

The Jaws of Life? What the hell happened? What's going on?

My chest tightened as I gasped for air, and my ribs ached

each time I sucked in a breath.

Please, someone tell me what's going on...

Reaching up, I touched my face. When I pulled my hand back, bright red blood shimmered across my fingertips— illuminated by the streetlights above.

Oh, God...

The sound of the metal door being pulled away made me jump, sending my mind into a sensory overload—crunching metal, sirens, and my own racing thoughts.

The firefighter carefully placed a neck brace on me. "Easy now."

He swiftly cut away my seat belt, and with the help of another firefighter, pulled me out of my seat and carefully placed me onto a backboard. Before I knew it, I was being whisked away and rushed into the back of an ambulance.

I grabbed the medic's shirt to get his attention. "What happened? Please tell me what happened?" I pleaded, needing answers.

He grabbed a needle out of a small drawer beside him. "You've been in a bad car accident. We're taking you to the hospital."

I gasped for air. "Wait. Mason. What about Mason?"

The medic frowned then grabbed a small vile of medication and a bag of saline. He turned back around and finally said, "He'll be taken to the hospital, as well. You can ask the doctor about him once we arrive."

Mason's face flashed through my mind as I blinked away tears. He was my boyfriend. I needed answers, and I wanted them now.

Licking my lips, the taste of iron and sweat latched onto my taste buds, making me gag.

The medic pulled me from my thoughts as he cut my dress and placed cold monitoring strips onto my skin, making me flinch.

My blond hair draped over my shoulder onto my chest. Grabbing a strand, I held it up, so I could see it more clearly. Panic set in when I saw the crimson-soaked tendrils. Seeing the blood was too much and sent me into a spiral.

Sitting up, I pulled the heart monitor stickers off and threw them down beside the stretcher. "I need to see Mason. I need to know he's okay."

"Ma'am, it's too late." He grabbed my shoulders. "We're already on our way to the hospital. Please calm down." He pushed gently, easing me back down. "Look at me," he said sternly.

Staring into his deep-set eyes, I tried to concentrate on my breathing.

"I need you to calm down before you injure yourself even more." His eyes narrowed. "Please just be still and let us help you." He sighed. "I know you're scared."

My shoulders relaxed for a moment. I exhaled slowly, trying to regain control of the fear that had taken over. The ambulance rushed down the blackened highway with sirens and lights on full force. The rocking of the ambulance made me nauseous, and my vision clouded again. I blinked, trying to focus.

"Ma'am, are you okay? What's wrong?" He cleaned the top of my hand with a cold alcohol wipe then inserted a needle. "Ma'am?"

There was a dull ache deep in my chest. "I'm...not... feeling..." I couldn't even get the words out before I closed my eyes and surrendered to the darkness consuming me.

No thoughts.
No sounds.
No pain.
Nothingness.

Chapter One

Kailyn

One Year Later
New York, NY

MY LIFE IN NEW York wasn't the same as before the accident. At the time, I had no idea my life would be forever changed after that weekend in Montana for my old college roommate's wedding. I was lucky to be alive.

I'd been on the heart transplant list for over a year because of the Atrial Septal Defect that I was born with. It had caused my heart to become enlarged, and my body was growing more tired each day. Everyone thought I was going to die the night of the accident because the stress of the collision on my already-weakened heart was too much. Reaching up, I grazed the bumpy scar, thankful I'd received a healthy heart, but sadly, someone else had lost their life. With death, there sometimes comes restored life, and I'd never take my second chance for granted.

Before the accident, I had everything I thought I'd ever wanted. A boyfriend who understood me and put up with my hectic schedule, a few close friends, a degree in Accounting from Columbia University, and a very high-paying job at one of the most elite fine dining restaurants in New York City. But all of that faded away before my eyes.

Mason lost his leg in the accident and would be spending the next fifteen years in prison on first degree vehicular manslaughter charges. Because someone died that night, my own guilt had been so heavy that I couldn't bring myself to look at the news of the accident nor hear anything of the court case after giving my statement. I had no choice but to put it all behind me because, if I didn't, the self-condemnation would cripple me.

Mason shouldn't have been driving, and I felt partially responsible for what happened. He told me he was okay and had only drank a few beers. Anger brewed within me as I thought about how stupid I'd been to believe him. I should've taken the keys and called a cab.

Hindsight is so haunting...

Walking down the sidewalk with a warm cup of coffee in my hand, I looked up into the sky, studying the towering skyscrapers. New York no longer felt like home. The busy city was all I'd ever known. So much so, I'd forgotten to slow down and actually enjoy it. Working eighty hours a week wasn't how I expected to live the rest of my life either, and since the company I'd worked so hard for had decided to sell, I decided to take the payout they offered and start over somewhere new.

A man in a dark business suit hurried past me, almost knocking me down.

"Excuse you!" I yelled at him.

Great. His inability to get to wherever he was going on time had caused me to spill coffee on my suit jacket.

Oh, this is going to stain!

Taking my jacket off, I made a mental note to drop it off at the cleaners on the way home, and I continued walking to work so I could pack up my things.

As I walked, I thought more about the night of the accident. Parts of it were still a blur, but I remembered Mason driving too fast down the winding, narrow road into town. I asked him to slow down, but he laughed and told me I worried too much. It was after midnight, and the headlights spilled out over the asphalt as he drove. The last thing I fully remembered was yelling at him as he crossed the yellow line and waking up to being pulled out of the mangled car.

Mason had written me a letter from prison telling me to live my life and never blame myself for what happened. He said he realized he shouldn't have been behind the wheel that night. *"I should've listened to you,"* he wrote. I'd always carry that burden of guilt in my heart, but I was working on piecing my life back together one day at a time. After receiving his letter, I wrote him back one last time, cutting ties, because we both knew there was no future for us with him being in prison for so many years.

It had been a year. A very long year of recovery and so many medications from the transplant I could barely keep up. The truth was, I couldn't exhaust my concerns on Mason while I was still worrying about my own wellbeing.

Once I arrived at work, I was greeted with hugs,

balloons, and flowers from my coworkers. *I'm sure going to miss them...*

Annette, the office secretary, approached me with a smile. She was like a grandmother to me. Her silver hair glistened under the low lighting and her neon green eyeshadow made me laugh. She was a vibrant soul with a large personality and had her own New York style.

"This is for you." She handed me a shimmering, silver spoon as a keepsake with the name of the restaurant.

The past few weeks were about tying up loose ends and making sure everything was in place for the new owners.

"Thank you for everything you've done to make this restaurant thrive." She frowned, scanning my half-empty office.

I pulled her into a hug. "Thank you, Annette. I'm going to miss you terribly." I glanced around to make sure no one was listening. "You know...you always were my favorite," I whispered.

"Honey, that's no secret. I'm everybody's favorite." She giggled, making me laugh.

After packing up, I made sure all the accounting files were together and ready to be sent to the auditor. This would be the last time I sign off of my work computer. It was bittersweet. My job here was done. Reclining back in my chair, I took one last look around my office as I thought about all the memories I'd made with coworkers who had become my family over the past several years.

Mentally prepared to leave, I turned the light off, closed the door, and knew exactly where I needed to be. If there was anything I learned after my accident, it was that life's too short to spend it working myself to exhaustion, so I was going to move to Montana to be near Leesa. I needed a change. More serenity and time with nature. Less time with busy city streets. A fresh start. A new beginning.

I was ready.

Chapter Two

KORBIN

Whitefish, Montana

U PON APPROACHING THE BAR, I noticed a new bartender I hadn't seen before.

"Pick your poison." She leaned over the counter, her cleavage spilling out over her tank top and shook her breasts in my face deliberately as she wiped down the bar.

Pathetic.

Glancing over her shoulder, I squinted at the row of glass bottles lined on the shelf and pointed to the Jack on the bottom row.

She smirked and pursed her plump lips. "A Fire kind of guy. Good choice." She turned to get a glass and poured the smooth, amber liquid.

Setting it on the coaster in front of me, she leaned over the bar again. "What're you doing later?" She smiled and licked her lips. "I get off in an hour."

"I'm busy," I scoffed, slapping a fifty dollar bill down onto the counter. "Keep 'em comin', darlin'."

She rolled her eyes and turned to serve a cowboy at the other end of the bar. Her ponytail swished back and forth as she walked away, and her short shorts hugged her hips perfectly. What the hell was wrong with me? She was practically serving herself to me on a silver platter, and I was turning her down.

I shook my head as she flirted with the other men across from me.

Classy.

Groaning in frustration, I twisted around on my barstool to watch the next band take the stage. A tinge of guilt and envy sparked through me as I watched them play. I used to play the guitar. Not anymore. Not since...

The bartender sauntered back over to me. "Are you sure you don't wanna get together after?" She reached out and touched my arm, pulling me from my thoughts, and I welcomed the distraction...somewhat.

She stared at me with hopes I'd say yes. However, I couldn't get past the heavy eye makeup and red lipstick on her teeth.

"No, thanks. I'm good," was all I said. I turned my glass up, finishing it in one gulp, then slid it back to her. "Another."

She exhaled a disgusted sigh and turned to grab the Tennessee Fire from the shelf. She poured it a little too quickly, and spilled some of it. After she handed the glass back, I swirled the alcohol a few times then took a gulp.

I raised my glass to her. "Thanks." I scrunched my eyes and leaned in to see her name tag more clearly. "Kayla."

"Whatever," she muttered under her breath as she walked away.

Looking toward the stage, I continued listening to the band play and tried to clear my mind, but no matter how hard I tried, I couldn't stop thinking about the ranch. Without Veronica, how was I supposed to keep it running by myself? It had been her passion—not mine. She was the brain and I was the brawn. We worked so perfectly together. All I did was planted and harvested crops, took care of the animals, and fixed things around the house. She'd always kept the bills paid. She'd always done the rest.

What the hell am I supposed to do to fix this?

Veronica's smile filled my thoughts. I still couldn't believe she was gone. Why couldn't she be here? Why her? She'd always told me the farm was the place she would grow old while rocking on the front porch teaching our grandchildren how to shuck corn and snap peas, just as she did our daughter. It was her sanctuary. Now she'd never be able to live out her dreams of growing old on the ranch with me or riding and caring for the horses with Kadence. She was taken suddenly and way too soon at only twenty-nine. She was my everything. She should be here.

Drinking wouldn't take my pain away, but it sure as hell helped numb it for a while. I downed the cinnamon liquor and winced as it burned my throat. Blowing out a breath, I covered my mouth with my fist, then swallowed again, waiting for the burning sensation to subside.

Turning to Kayla one last time, I contemplated the idea of taking her into the storage room, shoving her against the wall, and having my way with her. She stood there, practically begging me with her cat eyes, but guilt arose in me again.

Sighing, I stood from the stool and walked out the door, leaving the alcohol and needy bartender behind. It was time for me to go and wallow in my self-pity alone.

Walking into my dark and lonely country house, I flicked the lamp on by the front door and started a fire in the stone fireplace. I grabbed a bottle of whiskey out of the kitchen cabinet before making my way back to the front room and plopping down on the couch. Shadows danced on the wall as the soft glow of the flames lit up the objects around me.

Opening the bottle of whiskey, I chugged it until the burn was too much to handle. Veronica had been gone a year, yet the pain was still as bad as the day she died. I was tired of feeling like my heart was being ripped out of my chest over and over again with no end in sight. I was tired of feeling angry all the time, too.

When would I be able to smile or laugh again? Truly smile and mean it? Not just the fake smile I plastered on when Kadence was home or when everyone in the town decided to stop in to check on me and ask a million times if I am okay. "Bless your heart," they'd say. "I know this has to be tough on you and Kadence. Is there anything I can do to help?" I knew they meant well, but it was just too much sometimes.

My eyes stung with tears as I sat back against the soft cushions—on the same couch I made love to Veronica on many times before. Closing my eyes, I tried to remember every detail about her. The way she smelled like calming lavender, the way her laugh echoed through the empty house as we painted each room, her angelic voice that carried throughout the house as she sang while putting away laundry.

My face heated as I took another swig of the abrasive whiskey. I was angry at myself for being so weak. To everyone else, I was this perfect gentleman, a rich rodeo cowboy with fans around the world, but behind closed doors, I was weak and lonely.

Standing up, I stalked over to the large canvas portrait above the fireplace—Veronica's bright smile illuminated by the fire. Her chocolate brown hair fell delicately around her face, and her eyes were gentle, a honey-brown like I'd never seen before. I wished I could see that smile and kiss those full lips just one more time.

If only...

I blinked as tears escaped my eyes. My thoughts were scattered, and my mind was spiraling out of control. "You should be here, dammit!" I yelled.

Swallowing hard, I turned and threw the bottle across the room. It shattered against the wall—the dark liquid trickling down and soaking the floor below. "You should be here, Veronica." I dropped to my knees. "You should be here," I whispered between sobs. "I'm so sorry."

Chapter Three

Kailyn

Whitefish, Montana

STARING INTO THE DARKNESS through the open window, I took a deep breath of the clean mountain air, and sighed, perfectly content with my decision to move to the countryside. Pure blackness except for the stars. No lights, no tall buildings, no horns honking, sirens blaring, or people screaming. Just nature and peacefulness.

It was great being back in Montana with Leesa—or LeeLee, as I sometimes called her. After college, she moved back to Montana with her husband, Jake, and I stayed in New York to start my career as an accountant. Sometimes I wished I had gone with her instead of staying in the city.

Leesa walked into the room. "Are you settling in okay?" She held up a handful of towels and washcloths. "I forgot to stock the extra bathroom because it's hardly ever used, so I brought you these." She set them on top of the dresser.

I smiled. "Everything is perfect. Thanks again for letting me stay here."

"Of course." She shrugged. "This guest room needs to be used for something. Besides, having you here will be just like old times. Huh, roomie?" She laughed.

I closed the window and chuckled. "I guess you're right. Although…" I raised an eyebrow. "…Jake may not like that idea."

"Oh, don't you worry about him." She waved a dismissive hand. "He put up with our shenanigans at Columbia. I'm pretty sure he can put up with it for a few months here." She smiled.

Pulling the blanket down, I slipped under the covers. "I promise I'll be out of your hair as quickly as possible."

She walked over and took a seat on the edge of the bed. "Are you kidding? You're welcome here for as long as you need." She frowned, her eyes full of worry. "Are you okay, Kail?"

I laughed. "Yes, Leelee. I'm fine. I promise." I lied.

She turned her head and her lips formed a tight line. She didn't believe me. She knew me too well.

"Listen." I sighed. "I'm just ready for a fresh start. The past year has been hell for me back in New York, between recovering from my surgery, dealing with Mason, and leaving my job. All I want to do is put the past behind me." I reached out and touched her knee. "I'm going to start looking for jobs tomorrow, and I'll be in my own place before you know it," I promised, this time telling the truth.

She placed her hand on top of mine. "Okay, but there's no rush. You stay here as long as you'd like." She smiled.

"Goodnight. If you need anything else, just come get me."

"Okay, I will. Goodnight."

She turned the lights off and left the room, leaving me with nothing but silence and my own thoughts. I laid back and stared up at the ceiling as I wondered what was to come of my future. I was nearing thirty, and until the accident, I thought I knew what I wanted to do with my life. Nothing like almost dying to put things into perspective.

Growing up, my parents were all about money and power. As a child, I was lucky to eat dinner with both of them once a week. Usually, it was once every two weeks because they were buried in their careers as top business executives, or they were hopping on a plane to some exotic island. I'm pretty sure I was an *uh-oh* baby because they never had another after me, and I hardly ever saw them.

It was tough being an only child to parents who didn't want me. My childhood was a lot of me playing pretend in my room, by myself, while my nanny snuck her boyfriend into the guest house. Fixing myself cereal or microwaveable meals for dinner every day or the occasional Pop-Tart, if I was lucky.

I used to read to my stuffed animals every night, tuck them in, and give them kisses just like the moms and dads on TV did. Often, I wondered why my parents never did that, why they were too busy to tell me goodnight, or that they loved me.

After the accident, my life flashed before my eyes, and I saw myself falling into the same *workaholic* pattern as my parents. I knew I had to break the cycle, or I'd end up just like them. There was more to life than money, and it was time I ventured out to find my own happiness.

Yawning, I stretched as the morning sunlight peeked through the blinds. It was a new day. A new beginning. Sitting up on the edge of the bed, I rubbed the sleep from my eyes before throwing my disheveled hair into a pony and going into the bathroom to freshen up a bit.

Looking at myself in the mirror, I dabbed concealer below my tired eyes over the dark circles and finished putting my makeup on.

I groaned as I grabbed my pill dispenser and filled it with medications I had to take on a daily basis. *It won't be forever...* I reminded myself. Since the transplant, I'd been on so many medications that the bathroom counter looked like a pharmacy. I was anxious to get back to feeling like myself again.

But, first. Breakfast.

The smell of pancakes and fruit coming from the kitchen made my mouth water, and my stomach grumbled as I imagined the sweet, sticky syrup dripping down the stack I was about to devour.

Leesa stood at the stove, cooking. She glanced over her shoulder as I took a seat at the table. "Good morning."

Jake walked up behind her and kissed her on the neck. We were all inseparable at Columbia, and I just knew they'd end up married one day. Their love was about as genuine as any love could be, and he moved from the city just to be with her. Maybe one day I'd be lucky enough to have a man look at me the way Jake looked at Leesa. Even when Mason and I had first started dating, he never looked at me with such adoration.

Maybe I wasn't meant to have true love and happiness. I frowned as I thought about that.

Jake handed the newspaper to me. "Good morning, Kail. Sleep well?"

I smiled. "Like a baby."

"Good." He took a seat across from me.

Opening the paper, I turned to the help wanted ads. Cleaning lady, dog walker, nanny…the list went on. Nothing I could use my degree for, though. Five years of college for an Accounting degree, and the only jobs I could find here were low wage and part-time. The exact opposite of what I was looking for.

After tossing a few plump blueberries into my mouth, I finished scanning the list. Cashier, warehouse laborer, waitress…and then, finally…

Accounting/Financial Manager needed for the Hart of Country Ranch. Please bring resume to Korbin Hart at 1009 Hart of Country Ranch Cir.

I glanced up at Jake, who was taking a bite of his blueberry pancakes. "Hey, do you know anything about the Hart of Country Ranch?"

His eyes widened, and he shot a quick glance over in Leesa's direction before clearing his throat. "Yeah, it's about a thirty-minute drive from here." He took a sip of his coffee and set the mug back down. "Korbin is a well-known person in the community, the richest cowboy in Montana. Has several Rodeo Riding Championships under his belt." His lips formed a tight line, and he looked at Leesa again.

She gulped down an entire glass of orange juice and avoided eye contact with me. She almost looked nervous.

"Okay." I crossed my arms and glanced back and forth between both of them. "What's going on? Why are you acting so weird right now?"

"His wife died last year." He paused and took another bite of his pancakes. "I've heard he turned into a real jerk after her death." He shrugged. "That's all."

Setting the paper down, I sank back against the chair. *How sad.* Can't say I blame him. I'd probably be mad at the world, too.

I took a sip of my coffee. "Jerk or not, I need this job. It's the closest thing I can find in this small town that fits my experience."

"Are you sure?" Leesa sat down in the chair next to me. "I mean…working for Korbin may not be the best idea." She looked at Jake for a moment then back at me.

I laughed. "Come on, you guys. I'll be fine. I can take care of myself, and I'm sure I can handle a stubborn cowboy." I glanced at the ad again. "I'm going to go apply for it later today. It sounds perfect, and you know how much I love crunching numbers for others." I smirked, thinking back to our days in class when I'd always volunteer to work through the toughest problems.

"Yes, we know," they both echoed in unison, making me laugh.

They used to tease me all through college because I had an insane love for math.

I programmed the address into my phone and quickly finished my breakfast. My mouth watered as I savored the last bite of the fluffy pancake.

As I drove the country roads, I admired the mountains surrounding me. I'd only been to Montana twice before in my life, and that was for Leesa's engagement party and her wedding.

I'd forgotten how majestic the mountains were, nothing like what I was used to in the city. Montana was a beautiful place. Corn fields, mountain air, sunflower fields, and small town living. Just what I needed. The hustle and bustle of the city was part of me, and there were certain things I'd miss about it, but that life was no longer for me.

As I rounded a curve, my GPS lost service and stopped working. *Recalculating. Rerouting.* It kept repeating.

"Dang it," I mumbled as I tried to remember where it said my next turn was. I rounded another curve and turned right onto a dirt road.

I think this is it...

The red dirt turned to gravel about a quarter mile in. Trees surrounded me on both sides, forming a canopy of brilliant colors over my car. It was beautiful and peaceful. Then, a little bit of panic set in. What if this was leading me right to the house of a serial killer or something? What if I took a wrong turn? *I really should stop watching scary movies.*

Stop being dramatic, Kail. You're fine.

After about a half mile, there was an opening with a large entry sign that read:

WELCOME TO THE HART OF COUNTRY RANCH

Well, it's the right place at least.

There was a giant red barn up ahead on the right, I hadn't seen a lot of barns in my lifetime, being from the city and all, but this one was huge. A large garden with rows of corn stretched high toward the sky on my left, and a massive, white country-looking house with a bright red door and a wraparound porch set perfectly on a small hill straight ahead. It was breathtaking. The entire property was.

Swallowing down all my anxiety, I put my car in park, grabbed my portfolio and purse, and stepped out onto the gravel.

"Hey! Watch out!" I heard behind me.

As I turned around, two large pigs and a few chickens ran past me. The pigs were quite dirty, and one rubbed up against my leg, covering my expensive dress slacks in mud.

A little girl with pigtails ran by me. "Sorry about that. They escaped!"

Ugh. Great. Now I'm filthy.

I scowled as I bent over and tried to wipe the mud away, which only smeared it and made it worse.

"Ahem," I heard, also from behind me.

Great. What now?

I squeezed my eyes closed for a moment, then slowly stood up and turned. The man behind me had his arms crossed and flashed an amused grin my way. He stood there in his tight jeans, cowboy boots, and a t-shirt that hugged his muscles perfectly. He glanced down at my pants then back up at me. My cheeks warmed with embarrassment.

"Hi. I'm Kailyn." I reached my hand out, trying to conceal my awkwardness.

He shook my dirty hand and laughed. "Sorry about that, Kailyn. My daughter Kadence sometimes forgets to lock the animal stalls and cages after she feeds them." He leaned in and whispered, "Between you and me, I think she does it on purpose, so they'll like her better."

He made me laugh and that helped release some of the tension between us.

"I'm looking for Korbin Hart. I'm here to apply for the accounting position I saw in the paper." I reminded myself to smile, trying to forget I was standing on a farm covered in mud. "I'm sorry I'm such a mess." I laughed uncomfortably as I looked down at my heels and pants. Why in the world did I think it was a good idea to wear heels to a farm anyway?

He grinned. "You mean you don't normally show up to a job interview covered in mud?"

I smiled. "No, but once I did spill coffee on my white blouse before an interview."

Thank goodness for those little laundry stain wipes.

He chuckled and dropped his hands by his sides. "Well, Kailyn. It's nice to meet you. I'm Korbin, and if it makes you feel any better, I promise I won't hold the mud against you, since it wasn't your fault."

The embarrassment started to fade away. "Thank you. I appreciate that."

This man is Korbin? Oh boy.

His eyes were a dark, sapphire blue, and his lips looked very kissable. I usually didn't care for facial hair, but he wore the five o'clock shadow well. As I drank him in, my cheeks warmed, but this time it wasn't because I was uncomfortable. He made me blush just by looking at me.

Why does he have to be so gorgeous? Why couldn't he be a seventy-year-old man who is missing a few teeth, wears overalls and chews tobacco? Ugh. Just my luck.

"Do you have your resume?" he asked, pulling me from my thoughts.

"Yes, sir. Right here." I handed my portfolio to him. "Sorry about the muddy handprint." I scrunched my nose and shrugged.

He opened it, and his eyes shifted left to right as he read. He looked up at me briefly. "You're from New York? How'd you end up here?" He raised an eyebrow.

"I just moved here. I left my life in New York behind, so I could have a new beginning here. A fresh start." I wasn't sure why I had to say all of that. A simple, "Just moved here," would've sufficed.

Stop oversharing, Kail.

He nodded. "Fair enough. I guess the most important question is, are you staying long term? I don't need someone who's gonna run back out of state after only working a few weeks. I need someone reliable, someone who's gonna stick around and help me run this place." He gestured toward the farmland behind him.

Run this place? I thought I'd just be crunching some numbers for him and keeping all of his financial records and tax information updated. I didn't know I'd be *running* a ranch.

"No, sir," I stammered, unsure why he made me so nervous. Usually, I was a strong, confident woman with a clear head. "I'm staying here. As long as I can find a job, I won't be going anywhere. This is where I want to settle. City life just wasn't for me anymore." I smiled at him.

"Okay," he started. "First off, you'll have to lose the heels and invest in some boots. Second, the city clothes have to go." He raised an eyebrow, and his gaze scanned my body. "Although you'll be working in an office, you're still gonna get dirty. You'll need to buy some jeans and t-shirts. We don't dress up 'round here." He rubbed his chin and paused for a moment. "Unless we're going to church." He wiped some lingering sweat from his forehead. "Third, you've got the job. You start tomorrow morning at seven. Don't be late."

I stood there gawking like a deer in headlights.

I got the job? That's it? Applying for a job sure is different here in Montana...

"Ummm, okay then," I faltered. "Thank you for the opportunity." I shrugged. "I guess I'll see you in the morning."

He turned to walk away but stopped and turned back around to face me. "Oh, and Kailyn. Don't call me sir. It's Korbin. See you in the morning." He tipped his hat at me then walked back toward the barn.

Everything had gone so fast. That was the most unorthodox interview I'd ever had. I wasn't even able to respond to tell him whether I actually wanted the job or not.

Of course I need the job, but it would've been nice to have been able to accept an offer.

He just told me I got it. He didn't even tell me how much I'd be getting paid, what hours I'd be working, or any other information.

I stood by my car and scanned the property again as Korbin disappeared into the barn. He just turned and left me standing here. He hadn't given me a tour, shown me where I'd be working, or anything. He just left. So unprofessional.

Who does that?

With a huff, I got back into my car and headed to the store to buy a new wardrobe. Goodness knows I'd need one for this job. He made that very clear.

Chapter Four

KORBIN

AS I WALKED OUT of the barn, I turned around and glanced at the spot where Kailyn had stood hours earlier. She was going to be a train wreck. I mean, who wears heels and a dressy suit to apply for a job on a farm? I didn't know why I offered her the job so quickly other than the fact I was so damn stressed out and desperate I would've offered anyone the job, probably. Plus, she did have a few years of experience working as an accountant and had a degree from Columbia University. I just hoped she'd work out because I hated interviewing people, and I really didn't want to have to hire anyone else.

My mind wandered, and I chuckled softly as I thought about her muddy heels and pants and how flustered she'd looked. She was going to be a challenge because I was going to have to make a country girl out of her, for sure.

Kadence ran up behind me, grabbing my arm. "Who

was that lady from earlier, Daddy?"

"That's my new Business Manager. She's gonna help Daddy run the ranch." I picked her up and swung her around. "My goodness you're so muddy, darlin'. But still cute as ever." I put her back down and chased her around to tickle her.

She giggled as she ran and glanced at me over her shoulder. I stopped in my tracks and stared in awe. She took my breath away. Her cheeks were covered in streaks of mud, her dark-brown hair, chestnut eyes, and her bright smile reminded me so much of her mom. Her laugh echoed through me all the way to my heart.

After Veronica died, she was the only thing that held me together. If it wasn't for Kadence, I'm not sure I would've been able to get through the past year. She'd been my saving grace since losing Veronica. She was only seven, yet she continued to teach me more about love and life than I ever thought possible. She was six when Veronica died, and I only hoped she was old enough to keep memories of her.

Kadence stopped and turned to face me. "What's wrong, Daddy? Are you okay?"

I smiled at her. "Yes. I'm okay. You just remind me so much of your mama. She'd be so proud of you, kiddo." I tousled her hair.

She frowned, her shoulders slumped, and she looked down at the ground. "I really miss her."

Swallowing back my emotions, I said, "Me, too, sweetheart. Me, too." I tried reassuring her and took her by the hand as we made our way back to the house. "Now, let's go shuck some corn and get dinner started."

"Yes, sir!" she shouted, breaking away from me and running toward the house. She was such a free spirit. Again, just like her mother.

Kailyn

Leesa said she'd meet me at the local country western store to help me trade in my city girl attire. I'd lived the city life for so long that I had no clue what to buy for my new job.

We walked through the door, and I immediately headed toward the clothing racks. "There's so much flannel, and…t-shirts." I pulled a red flannel button-down shirt off the rack and held it against my body. "I can't wear this stuff…I mean… what is this?" I sighed and hung the shirt back up on the rack.

"It's called country living." Leesa laughed. "You better get used to it if you're going to be working for Korbin Hart. He's as country as they come." She grabbed a pair of jeans and cowboy boots off a nearby shelf. "You're not in New York anymore, Dorothy." She laughed.

Ha. Very funny.

It was going to take some time for me to embrace this new life. "You're right." I reached for the boots in her hand. "Ooohh I do love those boots, though. Thanks, Leelee."

"Whoa. Not so fast. These are for me." She pulled them back and placed them in the shopping cart.

"You do know we're here to shop for me, right?" I placed a hand on my hip. "You're supposed to be my wing-woman."

"I can still be your wing-woman and shop for myself." She smiled. "Now, let's go make you countrified…yee-haw!" She raised her hand over her head as if she were a roping cowgirl.

She pretended to throw the rope over me and pulled her arms back and forth as if she were *reeling* me in to her.

I rolled my eyes and brought my hand up to shield my face. "I don't know you right now. Remind me why I asked you to come here again?"

"Because you love me." She held a sky-blue, button-down shirt in front of me. "And because I'm your favorite friend in Montana."

I raised an eyebrow. "You're my only friend here."

She smirked. "Exactly."

"You're crazy." I laughed. "Give me that." I took the shirt from her and hugged it to my chest. As I looked down at it, I started to second guess this job.

I was not a country girl. What did I know about running a ranch? Ask me how to manage one of the hottest restaurants in New York? Sure. Ask me how to manage a ranch? Not so much.

"This is useless, Lee." I groaned. "This just isn't me. Am I making a mistake by being here and taking this job?" I blinked at her, pleading for answers.

Her eyes widened, and she stared at something over my shoulder.

I froze when I heard, "I don't think so." The voice was male and deep.

Crap. I remember that velvety, smooth voice. Korbin was standing only inches behind me.

My breathing quickened then I exhaled a slow breath.

Leesa pretended to look at the line of cowboy boots on the shelf beside her. I rolled my eyes. W*ing-woman, my ass...*

Slowly, I turned to face him and hugged the shirt even

tighter, my face heating with humiliation.

"Excuse me?" I scoffed.

His eyes were soft but guarded. "I said, I don't think you're making a mistake."

It was hard to comprehend anything he was saying while staring into his sapphire eyes. They looked just like the gem— blue, with specks of gray throughout.

If I didn't tear my gaze from his, I'd end up making a bigger fool of myself in the middle of the store.

He repositioned the cowboy hat on his head. "Look, I may not be the easiest man to work for, and God only knows what you've probably heard about me." He shrugged. "I know I can be a hard-ass at times, but as long as you do your job, we won't have any issues. Your resume is impressive, and I can train you how to run the ranch," he said matter-of-factly. I started to speak but he cut me off. "As far as your wardrobe goes, it's not really hard to dress for life on a ranch. Jeans, boots, t-shirts. That's all you need."

He grabbed a stack of white t-shirts off the rack and handed them to me. I followed him over to the boots and looked down at my feet, which were still covered in dried mud from earlier. "You a size seven?"

"Eight, actually." It shocked me he'd even taken a guess.

He handed me a pair of brown and teal cowgirl boots. "Okay. Here. Now go get some jeans and a few more t-shirts, and you're all set." His face grew serious, and he frowned. "Don't overthink things, Kailyn," he scoffed. "Something tells me you'll have no problem stepping out of your comfort zone for once." He flashed a roguish grin. "Who knows...you may even like it."

Once again, I was stunned, lost for words. I stood there,

my mouth opening and closing a couple of times as I tried to formulate a response.

Who does this guy think he is? He doesn't know anything about me. And is he giving me a Dr. Phil moment?

Finally, I found my tongue. "Thanks," I said curtly, snatching the boots out of his hands and placing them in my cart.

I did like the boots, though...

"Daddy, can I have these?" Kadence waved a small pair of pastel pink boots above her head.

He sighed and looked back at me with a sly grin. "How can anyone possibly say no to a new pair of pink boots?" He glanced back at her. "I guess. Go ahead and let Vern ring them up."

She skipped to the counter and chatted happily with the older gentleman at the cash register.

Korbin tipped his hat at me and smiled, this time a little less snarky. The curled sleeves of his flannel shirt pulled back, revealing the bulge of his biceps. Each muscle tensing beneath his tanned skin. Tiny hairs pressed against the surface from the dried sweat of a long, hard day on the farm. He was sculpted so perfectly, making me weak in the knees. I'd never felt this eager to be so close to someone so quickly, especially someone as frustrating and hard to read as he was.

"See you in the morning." He turned and walked up to the man behind the counter and shook his hand.

"Ahem." Leesa cleared her throat and bumped me in the hip with her cart. "I see someone is hot for the cowboy." She smirked.

I gripped the handle of my shopping cart and continued through the store. "Oh, whatever. He's my boss," I said, glancing over at him one last time.

She shrugged. "So what?"

"I need this job, Lee. You know that. I can't let anything jeopardize it." I picked up a few different colored t-shirts and threw them in the cart, cringing as I thought about wearing t-shirts and jeans every day instead of my business suits and heels.

What have I gotten myself into?

After finally deciding on a few more clothing items, Leesa and I made our way to the register to pay for our clothes. When Leesa was finished, I placed my items on the counter and pulled my wallet out. "You must be Kailyn." He flashed a toothless grin.

"Yes, I am." I stammered. "Nice to meet you."

He shrugged. "Small town. News travels fast. Everyone knows when there's a new pretty lady in town." His eyes wrinkled at the corners as he smiled. "I'm Vern. Short for Vernon." He extended a hand. "Welcome to Whitefish."

Gripping his hand, I shook it firmly. "Well, thank you very much." I smiled. "Nice to meet you, Vern."

I handed him my credit card.

"Oh. I'm sorry, darlin'. We don't accept cards here." He gestured to the large sign on the wall behind him:

Cash Only

He continued, "It's okay, though. It's already been taken care of."

My brows furrowed. "What do you mean?"

He put the clothing into bags then back into the cart. "Korbin already paid for it." He smiled. "He's a good 'ole boy."

"He did what?"

I'd just met Korbin, and he was already annoying me

with his control issues.

He winked. "Have a good one, darlin'." He then turned to straighten up some paperwork on the counter.

"Sure. You too." I grumbled to myself as I pushed the cart outside to the car.

Leesa unlocked the doors and opened the trunk. "Did I hear him correctly?"

"Yes. Korbin paid for my clothes. Who the hell does this guy think he is? I can afford my own clothes." I tossed my bags into the trunk and slammed it shut.

Leesa glared at me. "Well, technically..."

"Yes. I know." I sighed, realizing my bank account was dwindling, and I should've been thankful. It was hard for me to accept help from anyone since I'd been on my own for so long.

Leesa smirked. "That man has more money than he knows what to do with. Let him buy it if he wants to. Hell, ask if he'll buy me some clothes, too."

"Leesa, that's not the point." I shrugged. "He didn't even ask if he could pay for them. He just did it. I don't like feeling like a charity case."

She laughed and wrapped her arm around my shoulder. "Come on. Let's go back home, change into our PJ's way too early, put on some loud music, and dance around like old times while cooking dinner and drinking Sangria." She raised her arm and beamed with excitement.

I walked to the passenger side and opened the door. "I can't have alcohol anymore, remember?"

One of the many downfalls of my immunosuppressants. *No more wine.*

She frowned. "I'm so sorry, Kail. I forgot."

"It's okay." I shrugged. "Besides, if I *was* able to drink, it would have to be vodka instead of Sangria. Something tells me wine wouldn't be strong enough for me tonight." I laughed, but I wasn't kidding.

Back at the house, I slipped into my silky butterfly PJ's and joined Leesa in the kitchen. Pots and pans banged around, followed by a few choice words from Leesa.

"What in the world are you doing, woman?" I laughed. "It sounds like the house is falling down."

"Hey. Go over and put some music on the iPod!" she yelled over the commotion.

I picked the ipod up and scrolled through the playlist. "Ninety's or two thousand's?"

She closed the oak cabinet above her head. "Surprise me."

I smiled as I found the perfect song and pressed play.

"Ohhh girl! I haven't heard this in forever." Leesa grabbed a nearby spatula and held it to her mouth, using it as a microphone.

"Tootsee Roll," by the 69 Boys filled the kitchen and took us back in time to our college parties when we used to jam out and pretend we were cool.

Leesa threw a wooden spoon at me, encouraging me to sing. "Dip, baby..." She laughed.

We both twirled around the kitchen, gathering the supplies we'd need to make dinner. Laughing with my best friend again was much needed. Maybe living in Montana wasn't going to be so bad after all. I may not have been completely happy, but it was a start.

Startling us, Jake walked through the door, arriving home from work. "What in the world are you two doing?" He gave us a cautious grin.

Leesa sauntered over to him and put his hand on her hip. "Dip with me baby." She swayed her hips to the beat.

He shook his head at us. "You ladies have fun. I'm going to be in the office."

He kissed Leesa on the forehead then walked into the office, closing the door behind him.

Dinner was great, and my stomach was full. I couldn't remember the last time I'd eaten this well. Back in New York, I'd eat a yogurt or granola bar while working through breakfast, lunch, and dinner.

Glancing at myself in the bedroom mirror, I started to recognize the woman I used to be. I guess, until now, I hadn't realized I'd lost her.

I was content as I thought about how strong I'd felt earlier while dancing around the kitchen with Leesa. The past year had been hell for me. After my accident and surgery, my body had been so weak—still was at times.

Pulling the blanket back on the bed, I slipped underneath, making myself comfortable. My mind raced, and I wasn't sure I was going to be able to sleep, but I knew I had to try.

I set my alarm and turned the lamp off, before settling

into the feather-soft mattress. My thoughts drifted to Korbin and his piercing blue eyes as he tipped his hat and smiled at me—his eyes barely visible under the brim. Tomorrow was going to be an adventure. I hoped a good one.

Chapter Five

Kailyn

S TEPPING OUT OF MY car, I looked down at the boots Korbin picked out for me, my pale blue t-shirt, and jeans. "I can't believe I'm doing this. What was I thinking?" I mumbled to myself.

I started toward the massive red barn and stopped dead in my tracks when I saw Korbin shirtless and sweaty, tossing bundles of hay onto the back of an old pickup truck.

Holy mother of…

His skin glistened with sweat, and I involuntarily licked my lips. It was only seven in the morning, and he already looked like he'd been working for hours. He stopped for a moment and grabbed a bottle of water from a bench by the barn. Pulling his cowboy hat off, he tilted his head back and gulped the water down, swiping his arm across his forehead. After he set the bottle back down, he grabbed a white t-shirt off the back of the truck. The muscles in his back flexed as he pulled it over his head. Disappointment set in once his shirt was back on.

He looked at me then glanced at his watch.

No, I'm not late...

I realized how dumbfounded I must have looked, standing there in the middle of the field, gawking at the gorgeous specimen before me. Somehow I had to remind myself he was my boss, and my thoughts were very inappropriate.

He walked toward me, looking disgruntled. Working for him was going to be torture for two reasons—one fun, and the other...not so much.

"Good morning," I chimed up cheerfully.

"Mornin.'" He nodded. "Come with me, and I'll show you your office."

So demanding. Straight to the point and no messing around, I see.

I followed him into the barn and there were animals everywhere. I shook my head. Well, of course there are animals—I'm in a barn.

Why is he taking me in here instead of to my office?

After rounding a corner, he led me down a narrow hallway. "Here you go." He motioned for me to enter a small room. "Feel free to decorate or do whatever you need to do. If there are any supplies or anything you need, charge it to the company credit card that's in the top right drawer of the desk." He pointed at it. "Use it as you see fit. It's yours to keep."

I opened the drawer and took the card out. "Okay, thanks."

"Get settled in and familiar with the files. I'll be back later to start going over things in detail with you." He turned to leave.

"Wait." I frowned as I scanned the large room. "This is where I'll be working?" I sneezed into the bend of my arm.

There had to be some mistake. This wasn't an office—it was a dusty room, in the middle of a barn, filled with cob webs and hay. It just happened to have a desk and computer in it, but that didn't make it an office.

He raised an eyebrow. "Yes. Why?"

"Nevermind." I shook my head quickly, standing straighter. *You need this job, Kail.* "I guess I just thought I'd be in something a little less…I don't know…barn-like?" I shrugged.

"Look," he snapped. "This job isn't glamorous. It's hard work running a ranch, and if you don't think you can do it, then let me know now, so I can find someone else."

Great. I've been here ten minutes and already pissed my boss off. Hopefully I don't get fired on my first day.

Throwing my hands up, I waved them in front of me. "No, no," I said quickly, trying to dig myself out of the hole I'd just dug for myself. "It's fine. It'll be fine." I dragged my finger across the large oak desk and wiped the dust off on my jeans. "Thank you for giving me the opportunity."

I smiled, trying to remain calm. I didn't want my first day on the job to turn into a train wreck before it even started.

"Okay, great." He gave a curt nod. "Like I said earlier, get settled in and I'll give you a tour of the ranch when I get back."

He turned and walked out of the office, leaving me alone to ponder how in the hell I was going to make this work.

Plopping down in the black leather chair behind the desk, I coughed through the thick cloud of dust in the air. I made a mental note to stock up on sanitizing wipes and allergy meds. Leaning back, I sighed as horses clamored in their stalls and pigs snorted in their pens just down the hall from me.

Wonderful...How did I go from a five-star restaurant office with air conditioning and good lighting to an, "Away in a Manger" office, almost overnight? Oh, that's right; I chose to move here.

After taking a few minutes to get settled, I decided to go explore a little. Walking down the hallway, I rounded the corner, stepping back into the main part of the barn.

A large white horse immediately caught my attention. His coat reflected a shimmering silver glow under the low lighting, instead of white. He hung his head over the door and looked straight at me. He was the most beautiful horse I'd ever seen in person. Okay, to be fair, I hadn't seen many other horses, except for the few that the New York City police still rode while patrolling Central Park.

As I slowly approached the stall, I realized I'd never been this close to a horse before, and my heart thumped against my chest. Pushing my nerves aside, I decided to be brave since I would have to get used to my new office mates. Holding my breath, I closed my eyes and reached out to touch his nose.

"Get away from him," Korbin yelled from across the room, making me jump.

The horse backed away from me and reared up on his hind legs.

I shuffled my feet, backing farther away from the stall. "I'm...I'm sorry. I just..."

His face reddened and anger radiated from him. "You can touch any animal on this farm." He pointed at the horse.

"But not him."

Confusion consumed me in the moment, but I didn't ask any questions. "I'm sorry. I didn't mean to…"

I gave up trying to explain and dropped my head in defeat. I wasn't sure what I'd done wrong.

"Let's go," he snapped. "I'll give you a tour now."

He gestured toward the doors, and I followed meekly behind.

I wondered how many other ways I could get myself into trouble here. Probably a lot…

As we approached the house, a stone walkway lined with beautiful Mason jar lights led us to the front porch steps. *How creative.* Perfectly trimmed bushes lined the front of the porch, and clusters of rose bushes climbed up and around trellises—each one blooming in a vibrant red.

Cherry-red shutters lined both sides of each window, and a matching wooden door with a unique dandelion design etched into it was positioned perfectly in the center. There were six white rocking chairs that lined the front porch and a swing on one end.

Korbin stood on the top step. "Are you coming?"

"Yeah, sorry." I rushed to catch up to him. The scenery was eye-catching. "It's just the landscaping here is so beautifully crafted."

He stopped and turned around, making me slam into his chest. My breath hitched as his gaze hardened. "My wife did all of the decorating and planting herself. I've tried to keep it all up as she liked them."

I gulped. "Well, you're doing a wonderful job. It looks great."

He turned back around and opened the door, motioning

for me to go inside.

How gentleman like to hold the door open for me.

Walking inside, I was taken aback by the rustic, country charm of the house. Homes in the city looked nothing like this. The closest I'd ever gotten to a country house like this was watching *Little House on the Prairie* with my grandmother growing up. She had often told me she dreamed of getting out of the city to go live in the country where people really slow down and enjoy life. I smiled at the memory of my grandmother. She passed away from cancer when I was twelve, so I didn't get very much time with her.

Korbin snapped me back from my thoughts. "This is my house." His tone was indifferent. "If you need to use the restroom, get something to eat, or take a shower, feel free to use whatever you need." He pointed toward the kitchen then down the hall to the bathroom. "I'll make sure everything's fully stocked for you, just in case," he said curtly, turning to continue the tour.

This man doesn't play around or waste any time.

I nodded as I followed along.

"Got it," I grumbled under my breath.

As we passed the kitchen, I noticed it was bigger than my entire apartment back in New York. Marble countertops lined three walls, and there was an oversized kitchen island with built in cutting boards. My dream kitchen.

In the back room, there was a fireplace, and on the mantle was a row of pictures. From a short distance, I saw Korbin with his daughter and wife in one of the photos. They each looked happy, and Korbin was smiling in some of them. His face was relaxed and he looked happy; unlike the hard-as-stone man in front of me right now.

In one of the pictures, his wife was riding a beautiful white horse. It looked like the same horse Korbin had just yelled at me for touching moments earlier.

And then it hit me—that was *her* horse.

It all made sense now. That's why he flipped out about me touching him.

Without thinking, I picked the photo up to take a closer look. When Korbin noticed, he snatched it out of my hands and rubbed the glass with his fingers.

Standing there, looking lost for a second, he pinched the bridge of his nose and exhaled. "This is a small town, so I can only guess what all you've heard about me." He placed the photo back on the shelf. "I might as well go ahead and tell you, so you can hear it from me." He pointed to the row of pictures. "This is my wife, Veronica. She died a little over a year ago."

The pain in his eyes as he scanned the wedding photo on the mantle told me he was still heartbroken over the loss of his wife, but he tried to hide it.

He pointed at his daughter in one of the photos. "That's, Kadence." He smirked. "You already met her briefly."

Walking over, he grabbed another picture from the shelf, smiled down at his daughter's bright smile then set it back down.

His abrasive gaze from earlier softened as he looked back at me. "I'm sorry I yelled at you back there. I shouldn't have done that," he admitted, his tone more delicate than before. "Snowflake...he was my wife's horse. He's the only one off limits."

I'd known about his wife dying because of Leesa and Jake telling me, but I honestly had no idea about the horse.

Abruptly, he turned and walked to the back door.

I followed along. "I'm sorry about your wife," I said carefully, not wanting to upset him again, but not quite sure what to say. "I'll make sure I don't go near the horse again."

He ignored my comment and continued.

We walked through the back yard. A group of kids laughed and splashed each other in a nearby creek. They looked older, maybe around twelve or thirteen.

I giggled and pointed at them. "Are those your kids, too?"

"No, they belong to my farm hands. You'll see them around a lot during the summers and during the bulk of the planting and harvesting seasons." He pointed at a group of men across the field who were operating large pieces of equipment alongside rows of crops. "I couldn't run this place without each one of them. Some are teens who come to work for me helping them earn a little spending money, while staying out of trouble, but most of them are friends or family who've worked the farm for years." He looked around and inhaled deeply. "The Hart of Country ranch is the largest crop producing farm in Montana, and I plan to keep it that way."

Smiling, I glanced over my shoulder at the kids playing one last time before moving on. "What a fun and safe place for the kids to be able to come while their parents work."

He frowned. "It's been a struggle keeping everything going since Veronica died. I'm not gonna lie about that." He shoved his hands into his pockets and scanned the property. "I've tried running the ranch on my own, but I can't do it anymore." He sighed. "As much as I hate to admit it, I had to break down and ask for help."

"What about your family? Or hers?" I asked, hoping I hadn't overstepped.

He raised an eyebrow, obviously surprised by my forwardness.

"I'm sorry." I shrugged. "Sometimes I speak without thinking. Just trying to understand since I'm going to be taking on so much responsibility here."

It wasn't evident right away if he believed me, but hopefully that helped smooth over the fact that I just asked my boss personal questions about his family.

We continued walking. "They help where they can. Her parents don't come around much anymore because they say this place reminds them too much of her." He shrugged. "They're also much older and have retired in South Florida."

Disappointment crossed his face for a split second, then he quickly broke eye contact. Living at the ranch had to be just as hard for him because everything in the house, I'm sure, reminded him of her. The difference between him and her parents, though, was he couldn't run away from it.

He continued, "My parents help me a lot with Kadence because of my hectic schedule keeping up with the farm and my riding." He shook his head. "Although I don't like it, she spends the majority of her time with them because of it."

I gulped, feeling overwhelmed, but eager to help. "Okay. I'm going to do the best I can to help you run this place."

Something about Korbin made me want to succeed at this job. Maybe he wasn't such a hard-ass like everyone said he was. I was starting to think it was all a façade he'd put on to mask how he truly feels and to keep people from getting too close.

I wanted to help him, and I knew I'd have to dig my boots

in to do it—no matter what.

Chapter Six

KORBIN

Three Weeks Later

THE PAST FEW WEEKS had been a blur, trying to get Kailyn trained on the daily operations of the ranch.

I walked by the kitchen and overheard her on the phone with someone. Something was wrong and I didn't need her distracted with anything other than doing her job.

"It's fine, Mom. I'll be fine." She leaned against the counter. "I'm not homeless. Yes, I know I can't live with Leesa and Jake forever." She looked up and noticed me in the doorway. "I really can't talk right now. I have to go. I'll call you later." She hung up and set the phone on the counter.

I cleared my throat and placed my hat on top of one of the stools by the kitchen island.

She sighed. "I'm not sure how much of that you heard. I'm sorry." She shrugged. "Worried mom." She handed me a sandwich, trying to change the subject. "Lunch?"

"Thanks." I grabbed it off the plate and took a bite.

She returned to the sink to finish the dishes.

I didn't like the idea that she didn't have a place to stay. Maybe I could get her a room at the local bed and breakfast until she could find a place of her own...no, because everyone in town would badger her to death, asking questions about how I'm holding up, or if I'm eating and taking care of myself. It was just something they'd do. There was no privacy in a small town, and I needed to keep her away from there as much as possible.

I knew I'd probably regret this at some point, but I offered anyway. "My house is big enough." I put my sandwich down on the plate and grabbed a bottle of water from the refrigerator. "You can stay here until we can find you something reliable in the area."

What the hell did I just do?

She turned and gawked at me. "No, really. It's fine. You don't have to do that." She raised her hands in protest. "I'll be able to get a place of my own soon."

"That reminds me." I retrieved my checkbook out of the foyer table drawer, wrote her a check, and walked back to the kitchen to give it to her.

She glanced up at me and back down at the check a few times. "What's this?"

"It's your first month of pay."

I picked my sandwich back up and took another bite, finishing it.

Her eyes widened. "Wait." She blinked at me. "This is too much. That's too many zeroes for a month."

"Well, it's written in pen, so I can't erase it." I smirked. "I guess it'll have to do. Besides, there's no need to waste paper by writing another check." I chuckled. "Gotta save the trees."

She laughed at my dry humor.

"That's very nice of you, but I can't accept this." She tried to give the check back to me. "This is more than we agreed upon."

She was telling the truth, we'd agreed on much less, but I also didn't think she was going to last very long. She surprised me and deserved more for her time and effort.

"You've surpassed my expectations, and you deserve it." I pushed the check back to her. "You've worked your ass off here." I grinned discreetly. "You'll get your money's worth. Trust me."

Farm life was no joke, and so far, she'd done a great job with the payroll, expenses, scheduling, marketing, and everything else I had thrown her way.

She frowned. "We really need to have a talk about this." She held the check up. "Things like this is why your money is dwindling." She sighed. "You really have to stop being so check-writing happy." She crossed her arms and narrowed her eyes at me. "Do you even know how much money is in your account right now?"

There's the feisty accountant I hired. I smirked. "That's what I have you for."

"Ugh, this isn't a joke, Korbin." She slapped the check down on the counter. "You hired me to be your accountant, and that's what I'm doing. You have to listen to me and be more cautious with your spending. Yes, you bring in a lot of money each harvest and through the rodeo circuit and sponsorships, but all of that money won't last you forever."

I blinked at her. "Damn. I've had a lot of people upset

with me for various reasons before, but I can honestly say, this is a first."

She glanced down at the floor. "I'm sorry...I..."

"Look." I placed my fingers under her chin, pulling her head up, so she had to look at me. "You're right. I'll be more cautious of my spending habits and will consult you first going forward."

Dropping my hand from her chin, I forced it to my side. Touching her stirred feelings I wasn't ready for.

She sighed. "Thank you."

I rubbed the back of my neck. "If it really bothers you that much, then move into the house and help me with Kadence until you find somewhere to live. I could use someone to prepare meals and be here for her when I need to go out or have to work late on the farm." I paused, searching her face for any kind of reaction. "It would also help my parents out a lot." I shrugged. "Consider it overtime."

Her light-blue eyes softened, and I could tell she was actually considering it. For a moment, I wondered if I made a mistake. I wouldn't have done that for just any woman, so why her?

"You don't know me that well." She picked my plate up off the counter and placed it in the sink. "Why would you invite me into your house like this so soon?" She turned back around. "And to care for your daughter? I could be a crazy person for all you know."

I rolled my eyes. "Well, are you crazy?"

She looked horrified. "What? No." She shook her head. "Of course not, but that's not the point."

I smirked as I spilled everything I knew about her. "Let's see if I get this right. You've never been in trouble. Not even a speeding ticket. You were a nanny for six years. You grad-uated college with honors from one of the most prestigious schools in New York, and you were one of the top accoun-tants at a fancy restaurant in the city." I raised an eyebrow.

Her mouth dropped open and she cut her eyes at me. *If looks could kill…*"How do you know all that?"

"I had a friend check you out." I shrugged.

Like I'd have anyone working on my farm and handling all of my money that I didn't know.

Her eyes widened. "You did what?"

"Look," I started, unapologetic. "Nobody comes to work for me without being checked out first, and I have a daughter to protect." I stepped closer to her. "If I didn't trust you, you wouldn't be here right now." Changing the subject, I sighed. "I'm man enough to swallow my pride and admit I need you here, so will you please just move in and accept the check?"

She sighed and rested her hand on my arm. My body stirred again at her simple touch, and I was surprised by how easily she affected me.

She groaned. "Okay, fine. I'll do it. Besides, I'll get to sleep in a little longer since my office is in the front yard."

I laughed and instinctively caressed her cheek.

We both stood staring at each other. I wasn't sure what was going on, but there was something about Kailyn that en-thralled me. Her lips parted and I fought the urge to lean down and kiss her. I wanted to know more about her. See more of her. Be with her.

I dropped my hand and cleared my throat. "Well, when do you want to move in?"

What have I done? Guilt took over as I thought about Veronica and wondered if this was a good idea.

"Honestly, I don't really have much." She broke eye-contact and gazed out the window. "When I left New York, I left everything behind except for what I could fit in my car, which wasn't a lot."

I grabbed my hat off the stool and positioned it on my head. "That's okay. Bring whatever you have, and if you need anything else we'll get it." I turned to leave the room. "You can move in tomorrow morning."

Chapter Seven

KORBIN

A
FTER DINNER, WE SAT down in the office, so she
could present some of her findings to me. She'd
combed through the past year and found things I'd
missed which made me feel more at ease about hiring her. I
was the brawn of the ranch, not the brain of it all.

"It's getting late." I glanced at the time on my phone. "It's
already eight-thirty. Why don't you go on, so you can get
your things packed up for tomorrow? When you get here in
the morning, just come on into the house, and I'll show you
to your room."

She turned the computer off. "Sounds good to me. I'll
see you tomorrow."

She smiled at me, and for a moment, I didn't want her to
leave which scared the hell out of me.

I quickly stood and made my way toward the door before I ended up doing something stupid. "Have a good night."

"Korbin," she said, stopping me in my tracks.

Squeezing my eyes shut, I exhaled a slow breath. Hearing her say my name, had awakened feelings that had been dormant for a while now, and I didn't know why. I didn't want to feel this way about another woman. Not yet, anyway. It was too soon.

I turned to face her, keeping my expression neutral. "Yeah?"

"Thank you...for everything." She grabbed her purse and smiled.

I nodded once. "No problem. See you tomorrow."

Kailyn

"You're going to do what?" Leesa and Jake both asked, in unison, after I told them about my plans to move in with Korbin.

Jake dropped the pen he was holding onto the kitchen table. "You can't move in with a man you just started working for." He shook his head. "No way."

Leesa's eyes widened. "You can't live with Korbin."

Jake cut his eyes to her as if he was warning her to stop talking.

"Why are you guys acting so weird again?" I narrowed my eyes at them. "What's going on?"

Jake cleared his throat. "Nothing." He glanced back at Leesa. "We just don't want to see you get hurt."

I laughed. "I appreciate you both being so concerned,

but I'll be fine. Really. It's only temporary." I leaned back in the chair. "I can't stay here forever. I mean, you guys are still in your honeymoon stage. You don't need me hanging around." I pointed in the direction of the room I was staying in. "Plus, you're wanting to start a family, and I need to give you your space back." I picked my glass of water up and took a sip. "I'll be fine. I promise. I'm a big girl. I can take care of myself."

I wasn't sure if I was trying to convince them of that, or myself.

The thought of moving in with Korbin did make me nervous, but it also excited me.

"I don't know, Kail." Leesa frowned. "You know you can stay here as long as you need."

"I know, but I think this is the best idea. Living where I'm working will be a more efficient use of my time."

That, and the fact I'll get to see Korbin more.

Jake raised an eyebrow. "Okay. If that's what you want." He reached over and grabbed Leesa's hand. "We'll support you no matter what."

All through school Jake was like a protective older brother to me, and I loved that since I didn't have any siblings of my own.

"I know. I appreciate you so much for everything you've done." I smiled at both of them. "I'll be fine. I promise."

"Okay, then. It's settled." Leesa picked her glass up and clinked it with mine. "But you have to promise to check in with me at least every other day."

I rolled my eyes. "Okay, mom. Promise."

After finishing our talk, I went to pack up my things, and Leesa and Jake turned in for the night.

Zipping up my last suitcase, I sat on the edge of the bed and looked around the small bedroom. I felt like a gypsy with nowhere to go, no place to call my own. I was thankful for Leesa and Jake, and now for Korbin, for giving me a place to stay, but I knew I had to work really hard at the farm and start looking for my own place to live. I hated having to depend on others, and I needed to stand on my own again.

After stacking my belongings along the wall by the door, I turned the light off and tried to get some sleep. I would worry about everything else in the morning because I was mentally and emotionally exhausted.

KORBIN

I'd been sitting in my office, watching the fire crackle in the fireplace, for almost an hour after she left. I needed to be going through the details of my upcoming rodeo, but I couldn't concentrate. I couldn't stop thinking about her. She ignited a spark in me that hadn't been present in over a year. After my wife died, I was convinced I'd never feel this way again.

Glancing over to the edge of my desk, I smiled at the picture of Veronica, tucked away between a piece of glass and a thick, black frame. Picking the photo up, I touched my fingers to the glass and admired her for a moment. I set it back down on the desk and knew what I had to do. Grabbing my jacket and hat off the coat rack, I headed for the bar about a mile down the road.

A tall, curvy, blond bartender greeted me. Shelly was her name. She was well known throughout the town and not for good reasons.

"Hey, Korbin. What can I get for ya?" She placed a coaster down on the bar in front of me.

I pointed to the large glass bottle on the end of the shelf behind her. "Fireball."

She licked her lips. "Mmmm. Man after my own heart."

Not tonight, Shelly. You can save your flirting for someone else. What is it with the needy bartenders in this town? I just want a drink.

She set a small glass down in front of me.

Watching her pour the sixty-six proof atomic sedative, my mouth watered for it. In one fluid motion I picked it up, kicked it back and welcomed the burn.

My best friend Max, came up and slapped me on the back as I set the empty glass on the bar in front of me and motioned for another.

"Hey, man! What's up?" He squeezed my shoulder. "Long time no see." He sat on the stool beside me.

Max was also the doctor who tried to save Veronica the night of the accident, so he had seen me at my worst. We grew up together from our days of mud pies, GI Joes, fast cars, and chasing girls. We'd been through it all together.

"Yeah. I've been busy with the ranch. Finally got some help, though." I stared absently at the crowd of people on the dance floor. Their half-drunken attempts at dancing the Electric Slide was not at all appealing.

It was the same old, same old, night after night in this town. Everything was so predictable.

Max leaned over the bar and lifted his hand to catch Shelly's attention again. "A beer please, darlin.'" He winked at her. "You know what I like."

She smiled and bit her lip. "Sure thing. Comin' right up."

Oh, please. I rolled my eyes at the exchange.

Max folded his hands on the bar in front of him. "So, tell me about this new help of yours."

Glancing down at the amber liquid in my glass, I sloshed it around a few times. "She just moved here. She has a master's degree in accounting and I think she's gonna be okay." I smirked. "She's a city girl, though, so she doesn't really have a lot of knowledge about farm life."

I chuckled as I remembered how disheveled she looked in her mud-covered fancy suit the first day I met her.

Picking the glass up, I swirled it once more, watching the alcohol circle inside before bringing it to my lips for another taste.

A taunting grin spread across his face. "Oh, hell." He folded his arms across his chest. "You like this girl."

I scoffed. "Whatever, man. It's not like that." Although, I knew he was right.

Her tantalizing blue eyes and sun-kissed blond hair flashed through my mind, and I couldn't forget how sexy she looked in tight jeans and cowgirl boots.

He shook his head. "You can deny it all you want, but I haven't seen that look on your face in a long time. Not since..." He stopped himself and cleared his throat. "Sorry."

I groaned and tossed back another shot. "I haven't known her very long. Plus, I really need help at the ranch, and I can't be sleeping with an employee."

A shadow passed over his eyes. "Man, don't do this. Stop punishing yourself and just be happy. Veronica would want you to be." He took a swig of his beer and set the bottle down on the coaster. "She'd want you to move on. It's been over a year now. Remember, you're still here." He raised an eyebrow and tilted his head. "Stop torturing yourself."

Great, that's all I needed. My best friend feeling sorry for me. I sighed. Maybe he was right…again. She'd only been gone for a year, though. It felt wrong.

"You know, it really doesn't matter anyway. Like I said, she's an employee." I shook my head. "I can't mix business with pleasure."

Oh, but how I wish I could.

He smirked. "Oh, you can definitely mix business with pleasure." He jumped down from the stool and threw a fifty dollar bill on the counter.

"Yes, I forgot." I rolled my eyes. "You're a big time doctor who sleeps with his nurses. You're the master of mixing business with pleasure." I laughed.

"Damn right!" He slapped me on the back. "Now… come up on stage and play a set with me. It's been too long."

I glanced up at the stage and back to Max. "No, thanks. You go ahead. You know I haven't played since Veronica died. I have no desire to play anymore."

The truth was, a small part of me did want to play again. To hold the neck of the guitar in my hands and feel my fingers against the frets, but it hurt too much. I just couldn't do it anymore. Not without her.

"Alright, then." He sighed and grabbed my shoulder. "If you change your mind, just come on up. See ya later, Korb."

He disappeared into the back to get ready to play.

I threw down another fifty and left. I'd had enough con-fusion for one night. It was time to go home and get some sleep.

Chapter Eight

Kailyn

THE NEXT MORNING, I said my goodbyes to Leesa and headed for the ranch—my new temporary home. Hopefully, my last temporary home until I buy a place of my own.

Korbin was waiting for me by the house when I pulled up. He leaned against the front porch post, his arms crossed over his chest. I'd never been into the cowboy type, but I was starting to think I could learn. Taking a deep breath, I gave myself a quick pep-talk in the rearview mirror and stepped out of the car.

Korbin walked over to help me carry my things in. He scanned the back seat and raised an eyebrow. "This is it?"

"Yep." I shrugged. "I told you I didn't have much."

Without another word, we walked into the house and up the stairs. Again, I couldn't help but admire how beautiful the house was. I ran my hand along the smooth, polished wood railing as we ascended the stairs. He stopped in front of a door about halfway down the hall.

"This will be your bathroom. Feel free to do whatever you want to it. It's yours while you're here." We continued to the room across the hall, and he opened the door. "This is your bedroom." He switched the light on and set my bags down beside the large king-sized bed.

I set my purse down on the nightstand and surveyed the room. "Are you sure about this?"

"Yes." He walked to the window and opened the curtain. "You can stay as long as you need to." He grinned. "Kadence knows you're here, and she's excited to have someone else to talk to besides her boring dad."

His face lit up when he talked about Kadence, and I could tell he was a great father.

Walking to the window, I glanced at the creek behind the house. Rows of trees lined most of it. Korbin walked up behind me, and I froze. He smelled delicious, and I had to fight the urge to turn around and nestle my head against his chest.

"It sure is beautiful here," I whispered, trying to concentrate on the scenery instead of the way my body was reacting to being near him.

He leaned in closer. "It sure is."

My breathing stilled.

Needing some fresh air, I reached up to open the window, but he reached up at the same time, his hand practically grabbing mine. Looking over at him, his eyes wandered from my eyes down to my lips. My heart raced. The chemistry between us radiated through my entire body. His chest rose and fell with each quickened breath. I bit my lip and turned so that I faced him directly.

His seductive, smoldering eyes were fixated on mine. He caressed my cheek and leaned down closer to me. After a moment, he dropped his hand and squeezed his eyes closed. When he reopened them, his eyes were dark and solemn. The spark gone.

He cleared his throat. Moment over. "I'll let you get settled, then we'll get started on the accounting files when you're done." He turned and walked out the door, closing it behind him.

I walked to the bed and fell back onto it, feeling confused. *What just happened?*

After taking a few minutes to replay what had just happened, I stood back up and forced myself to go out to the barn, to my office, to get some work done. The more distance there was between us, the better, and I had to occupy my mind with something else.

KORBIN

I groaned as I paced the floor of my master bedroom. Why was I so attracted to Kailyn? If I'd known I was going to respond to her that way, I never would've hired her.

What the hell is wrong with me?

I was torn between the attraction I had toward Kailyn and the love I still had for my wife. I still thought about Veronica every day. Her smile and the sound of her laugh when I'd wrap my arms around her and kiss her neck.

Looking up at our wedding photo hanging on the wall above the bed, I dropped my head and sighed. I had to go back out and face her. I had to learn to not only work with this woman but learn to live with her while she was staying in a room next to mine.

As I swung the door open, Kailyn was walking down the hall toward the stairs. She peeked at me over her shoulder, and I saw it then—the same fire in her eyes that radiated through me earlier. I leaned against the door frame, my eyes zoned in on hers. Sexual and emotional frustrations took over as she disappeared around the corner and down the stairs. There was something about Kailyn and the way her body and mood responded to mine. It was as if we were deeply connected in some way—our energy feeding off one another, completely taking over our emotions.

Chapter Nine

Kailyn

AFTER HOURS OF TYPING in data for the ranch and organizing most of the finances for the month, my mind needed another break, only this time, the break I needed was from crunching numbers, not Korbin. To be honest, I wasn't sure which one made my head hurt worse.

Walking out of the office, I realized there was a room in the back that I hadn't noticed before. Unable to quench my curiosity, I opened the heavy wooden door. I'd have to be fast, I thought, as I quickly glanced over my shoulder to ensure Korbin wasn't around. The last thing I needed was him yelling at me again, but if I was going to work the ranch, I needed to know what the room was.

"No way." My jaw dropped as I found myself staring at a huge mechanical bull in the middle of the room, surrounded by mounds of hay.

Korbin's voice behind me made me jump. "Why don't

you take him for a ride?"

Seriously? How does he keep sneaking up on me like this?

"Korbin! I'm-I'm sorry," I stammered. "I was just…" But I had no good excuses. The truth was that I wasn't able to contain myself from snooping.

He chuckled, thankfully not looking angry like when he yelled at me about the horse. "It's okay. This is where I spend most of my time training for the rodeo." He walked over to the bull then turned back to me. "Come on," he challenged, wanting to see if the city girl could hack it, no doubt.

"No." I shook my head. "I don't think so. I'm a city girl, remember?" I said, adding fuel to the already challenging fire in his eyes. I fed right into his game, and now, I had no choice but to prove to him I could do it.

He held out his hand and nodded. "It's okay." He grinned. "We'll take it slow at first."

I gulped and stepped closer to him—only inches from the bull. My body shook with fear and my knees almost buckled. "I don't know what to do."

He raised an eyebrow, obviously amused at my discomfort. "That's okay. I'll show you." Grabbing my hand, he helped me up the step stool. "Okay, lean forward and throw your right leg over his back," he prompted.

Doing as he instructed, I settled myself onto the back of the bull and remembered what Jake and Leesa had told me about Korbin being one of the most successful bull riders in the world. Leesa said he'd been in competitions since he was old enough to ride a sheep, and he'd never looked back since. Most of the money he'd earned was from winning so many competitions. I tried to imagine what it must feel like for him when he first mounts a real bull during a competition.

He grabbed a rope and slowly wrapped it around my hand. "Now, you have to make sure you hold onto this and keep your other arm up in the air at all times."

He moved the stool out of the way and came closer, placing one hand on mine and the other on my thigh. "I'm gonna turn it on now, but we'll start off slow, okay?"

My heart raced, and I wasn't sure if it was because I was riding a mechanical bull or because Korbin was touching me. Probably both.

A part of me was intrigued by the bull, but the biggest part of me was terrified. "Okay," I whispered.

He walked over to a small desk in the corner and flipped a switch. "It has a thirty second delay, so just hold on and do what I told you. I have it on the lowest setting."

My breath quickened, and my heart pounded against my chest as he turned a small knob on the panel a quarter turn and joined me back over at the bull.

His brows furrowed. "Hey," he said calmly, sensing my fear. "Do you trust me?"

As soon as he said that, I realized I had to trust him. I wasn't sure why, but something about him calmed me— made me feel safe.

I didn't hesitate. "Yes."

His expression softened, and he smiled. "Okay. Good. Now, take a deep breath and close your eyes."

"Close my eyes?" Riding the bull was scary enough, and now, he wanted me to close my eyes?

"Trust me."

I sucked in a deep breath and exhaled slowly, closing my eyes. *This is crazy.*

He placed one of his hands on my thigh like before and

one on my lower back. I squealed as the bull moved beneath me.

It bucked slowly, and I tensed as it rocked me back and forth.

"It's okay. Just relax into it." The sound of his voice provoked chills across my body.

As I relaxed, my body swayed with each movement.

"There you go," he praised as he continued to instruct me. "Squeeze your knees together and square your hips and shoulders with the bull."

My eyes remained closed, and I tried to concentrate on my form and the sound of his voice.

"You see, Kailyn. Riding a bull is a lot like dancing." His hands rubbed against my body as he moved along with me. "Let the bull lead, and you follow. Mimic every move it makes, and stay in sync with it."

Doing as he said, a sense of pride washed over me. Mechanical or not, I never thought I'd be on the back of a bull.

Korbin's prolonged touch enthralled me. Another surge of adrenaline shot through my veins, and I squeezed my thighs tighter against the bull to relieve the ache at my core.

KORBIN

I stepped back to the corner where the control pad was. She'd taken me by surprise with how well she was doing, so I decided to take it up a notch.

"Korbin!" She opened her eyes in a panic. "Where are you going?"

"You've got this, Kailyn. I'm right here. Just concentrate and feel the bull as I told you. Remember. Just dance," I reminded.

Watching her on the bull was intoxicating, and I enjoyed it way too much. Seeing her overcome her fears and fully trust me to help her was sexy as hell.

Her chest rose as she inhaled deeply. "Just dance," she repeated with a nod. "Just dance." She exhaled slowly.

Her body rocked back and forth against the bull, her hand still gripping the rope and her other hand up in the air just as I told her. I adjusted myself as I watched her buck and spin. I turned the dial to speed it up a little, and to my surprise, she kept up with it. Her hair whipped around her face, and she peered at me through the blond locks that covered her eyes. The more I watched her, the more turned on I was. I had to get her off.

I cleared my throat as my mind wandered. *Off the bull…*

"Korbin!" She screamed, pulling me from my thoughts.

Before I could get back to her, she slipped off and landed on the hay below.

"Kailyn!" I quickly switched the bull off and ran over to her. "Are you okay?" I bent down and lost my balance, barely catching myself as I fell on top of her. She made an *oof* sound then I heard something come from her mouth I didn't think I would. "Are you…laughing?"

She giggled and looked up at me. "I can't believe I did that. What a rush!"

She blew a strand of hair out of her face, and I gazed into her sky-blue eyes. The excitement in them took my breath away.

I chuckled. "I told you you could do it."

She laid beneath me on the hay, disheveled hair and all. She was radiant and gorgeous. The shy city girl I met weeks ago already seemed so different. I never thought she'd fit in here or even try to live the country life, and now that she was, I liked it a little too much. Glancing at her lips, I fought the urge to kiss her. I wanted to. Badly. But I couldn't.

I stood and extended a hand to her. "Come on. I'll help you up."

For a moment, she looked disappointed. She grabbed my hand and stood in front of me. After dusting herself off, she looked up at me and placed a hand on my chest. "Thank you, Korbin. I never thought I'd say this, but I really enjoyed that." Her eyes narrowed. "I have no clue how you do that on a real bull."

I caressed her cheek with my hand, loving the feeling of her porcelain skin beneath my fingers. "Ridin' isn't easy, but the adrenaline and the pride I feel when I hear the buzzer makes it worth every second."

She trembled beneath my touch. I resisted the urge to pull her to me, settling for stroking her hair. "You've got hay in your hair." I chuckled. "You're a true cowgirl now."

It felt odd—laughing again, but I kind of liked it. Darkness had taken over my life for the past year, but I was starting to feel again.

I swept her hair back and tucked the piece of hay behind her ear. "You wear it well." I grinned. "Country looks good on you."

After feeding all the animals and making sure the barn was locked up, I tried my best to forget what had happened earlier. It was dinnertime. Maybe that would distract me from Kailyn.

I showered quickly, got dressed, and headed down the hallway toward the stairs.

The bathroom door flung open and steam rolled out. We collided as Kailyn attempted to rush by me. To steady her, I grabbed her arms and my hands slid down her still damp skin.

"Korbin!" She brought a hand up to her chest. "You scared me. I didn't know you were back in the house yet." She tugged her towel up self-consciously over her breasts.

I cleared my throat and dropped my hands from her arms. "I'm, ummm. I'm sorry I scared you." My body betrayed me at the sight of her, and I tried to gather myself. "I came in early so I could cook dinner tonight."

We stood in the hallway, her in nothing but a towel. Her wet hair draped across her cheeks and clung to her shoulders. Little beads of water rolled down her neck and chest and disappeared between her breasts. She was stunning.

She broke eye contact and cut her eyes toward the bedroom door. "It's okay. I'm going to go get dressed now. I'll meet you downstairs for dinner."

She scurried off like a twelve year old who still believes boys have cooties, closing the door behind her.

Swallowing back my emotions, I gave myself a peptalk and a friendly reminder as I headed downstairs to start cooking.

She's your employee. Don't sleep with your employee.

Kailyn walked into the kitchen. "What smells so delicious?" Her hair was still damp from her shower, and my mind went right back to seeing her in a towel—her bare shoulders glistening under each water droplet.

Shaking that thought out of my head, I turned back to the oven, trying not to stare.

"Homemade lasagna and veggies from the garden."

She had on a t-shirt that hugged her curves perfectly and a pair of black leggings. How could a woman look so sexy in a t-shirt and leggings? One of the things that impressed me the most about Kailyn was that she never tried to capture my attention, she just did. While traveling around the world for rodeos, women had always flashed themselves in front of me or thrown themselves at me to get my attention, but Kailyn hadn't. She truly didn't know how beautiful she was and that made her even more attractive.

My body began to stir again, so I turned away from her and grabbed some silverware from the drawer to my right.

"I can't wait to taste it." She inhaled deeply as she walked over to where I was standing.

My mind began wandering again as I imagined what her kiss would taste like, but then I swallowed hard and, again, pushed the images out of my head.

She pulled two plates from the cabinet and set them on the table. "Can I help with anything?"

I pointed to the counter. "You can make the salad and put it in that bowl."

She grabbed a knife to cut up the veggies for the salad.

The silence in the room was deafening.

"I know what's missing." She grabbed her phone. "Music."

She hooked it up to the sound system that was wired for the house. Each room had its own speaker, and it could also be used as an intercom.

Music filled the house as she made her way back over to the counter. "Just for you." She smiled.

Her hips swayed back and forth to the beat as she danced while cutting. Luke Bryan had never sounded better than in this moment. I chuckled under my breath. Her care-free spirit made me jealous. I longed to feel that way again. Despite the huge part of me that still grieved, that may always grieve, there was a part of me that wanted to be truly happy again. Between having to bury my wife, raise Kadence on my own, and run the ranch on my own, I was spent. Tired. Overwhelmed.

Maybe I was ready for a change, but there was still one problem. She was my employee, and I really needed her to help me run the ranch.

She tossed the salad and set the bowl down on the table. "All done."

We sat and ate without even speaking while music still filled the room. I had so much to ask her, but I couldn't get the words out. I wanted to know everything about her.

Kailyn

I stabbed a piece of the cheesy lasagna with my fork and took a bite, savoring the flavor. A sexy, hard-working cowboy and single father who was also a great cook? Yeah, he was a catch for sure.

*But, he's your boss…*I reminded myself.

The silence made me uncomfortable, so I broke it. "Where's Kadence?"

He relaxed at the mention of her name. "She's with my parents. She stays with them a lot during rodeo season."

I smiled. "I can't wait to see her again."

"She's pretty awesome." He smiled, loosening up a bit.

"More water?" He noticed my glass was almost empty.

I held my glass up. "Sure."

He retrieved the carbonated water from the refrigerator and refilled it.

As he finished pouring, his sapphire eyes caught my gaze then shifted curiously down to my lips.

After nervously biting my lip, I tilted the glass against my mouth and took a sip.

He sat there, watching me, making me squirm. I wanted to reach out and touch him. Kiss him. No, I wanted him to take me right there on the kitchen table. I'd never felt so strongly about a man I barely knew, but I couldn't help feeling this way toward him. My body and mind switched to autopilot whenever he was near, and I had no control.

He stood and stepped away then placed his glass of whiskey on the counter. "It's getting late. I better clean up and head to bed."

I took another sip of my water then stood from the table to help him. He was so hot and cold, and I didn't like it.

He wouldn't even look at me. "I've got it." Instead, he gripped the edge of the counter with both hands and dropped his head. "Why don't you go on to bed and get some rest?"

Okay, then…

He wasn't really asking. That was more of a demand.

Walking into my room, I shut the door behind me. I collapsed onto the bed, confused as to what had just happened. We were having a perfectly good time, then it got awkward between us again. I knew he felt the same way I did; I could see it in his eyes, so why was he making it so hard for us to connect?

You know, if he isn't going to make the first move, then maybe I should. Maybe he's afraid to make a move because he's my boss...

I understood his hesitation if that was the reason because I had felt the same way at first, but the more I was around him, the harder it was becoming to pull away from him.

Jumping off the bed, with a sudden boost of courage, I headed for the door, swinging it open, and slammed right into Korbin's chest. "Korbin, I was just coming to..." I started, wondering why he was standing outside of my room, or how long he'd been there.

His eyes searched mine for a moment, and he ran his hand through my hair. "I'm so damn tired of pretending and fighting this...whatever this is." He sighed. "I've spent the last year in hell, pushing everyone in my life away, and I don't want to do that anymore." He backed me further into the room. "I want you, Kailyn. Right now," he crooned. Then before I could say anything, his lips crashed down on mine with a tantalizing kiss that rocked me to my core.

He pushed me over to the bed. My brain told me to stop him, but my body and heart had other plans. I jerked his shirt up over his head and threw it on the floor. He did the same with mine and looked down at my chest.

My scar!

The rough, pink flesh left a trail down the middle of my chest. If it weren't for the heart transplant I wouldn't be alive, and I knew that, but I hated that ugly scar and wished it would disappear. It was a constant reminder of the day of the accident. With over a hundred thousand recipients needing organs, I was thankful I got mine when I did, though.

The day I found out about my heart defect, I wasn't sure if I'd ever receive a heart, and every day was like living with a ticking time bomb in my chest. With each passing day, I could feel the life being drained from my body.

Korbin glanced at my scar then back up into my eyes. He was curious, but he didn't ask any questions. Instead, he traced the scar lightly with his fingers. My first reaction was to reach up and stop him, but he grabbed my hand.

"Don't." He pushed my arm back down to my side. "Don't be ashamed of something that's a part of you and your journey through life."

His words assured me and turned me to putty in his hands. Him saying that meant a lot to me.

Tears formed beneath my lashes, and I squeezed my eyes closed to stop myself from crying. He was the first man to see my scar, and I'd been worried about any future man in my life being turned off by it. It shocked me how gentle he was being and how he managed to make me feel sexy and less self-conscious about it.

"Thank you." I sighed.

His lips and tongue found mine once again as he laid me back onto the bed. He pressed his thigh between my legs, and I laced my fingers behind his neck. He kissed along my jawline over to my ear and sucked gently on the one spot below my ear that sent my body into a frenzy.

His words echoed through my mind over and over again.

Don't be ashamed of something that's a part of you and your journey through life.

I'd never really looked at it that way before and having grown up in a big city, with rich parents who were all about their image, I was used to everyone around me making me feel like I always needed to be *perfect* in order to be a beautiful woman.

Although feelings had developed quickly, I was falling for Korbin.

Leesa said she knew she was going to marry Jake the first day she met him. They were engaged after two months of dating and have been happy ever since. I'd never really believed in love at first sight, but I knew in my heart my feelings for Korbin were real. There was no doubt about that. I only hoped his feelings were as strong.

He stilled on top of me. "What's wrong?" I asked taken aback by his sudden disconnect.

"Korbin?" Searching his eyes for answers, I reached up and touched his cheek. "If you aren't sure you want to do this, we don't have to."

He interrupted me. "It's not that." He sighed. "You're the first woman I've kissed or touched like this since Veronica." He rolled off of me and onto his side. "I'm just trying to process everything and figure it all out," he said gruffly.

It was hard to imagine what he was going through, so I wasn't sure what to say to him, but I wanted to comfort him somehow. "It's okay." I touched his arm. "We probably shouldn't be doing this anyway."

He sat up abruptly. "No, that's the problem. I want to do this, but I can't get my mind off of the guilt I feel for betraying

Veronica."

Without hesitation, I sat up beside him. "Korbin, you are not betraying Veronica. When someone we love dies a part of them will always live on with us, but you have to remember, you're still here. Your life doesn't stop." His jaw tightened as I spoke. I wasn't sure if I should stop or continue, but I had to get through to him one way or another. "Just because you move on with your life doesn't mean you'll forget about her or not love her anymore." I placed my hand on his chest. "Veronica will always live on in your heart and through Kadence. She'll never be forgotten, and I'd never ask you to forget about her or stop talking about her."

His body relaxed. "You're one hell of a woman, Kailyn North," he crooned. The playfulness he'd shown earlier had returned. "I'm not sure how you ended up here, but I'm so damn glad you did."

I rubbed his thigh. "Me, too."

Taking my face in his hands, he kissed me again and laid me back leaving a trail of kisses down my neck. He sucked on my sensitive skin, making me squirm. Tightening my arms around him, I dragged my nails across his back. He moaned into my ear and quickly pulled my pants off. After settling back between my legs he ground himself against me while his mouth explored my body. He positioned himself over me and entered me in one long thrust.

Twisting the sheets around my hands, I threw my head back and bit my lip to keep from screaming as he stretched me.

KORBIN

My mind had been a jumbled mess since Kailyn arrived, but one thing I knew for sure, I was drawn to her and not just physically. Somehow she'd managed to get through to me in ways I'd been able to ignore from others.

As I looked down at her, all I saw was her face, not Veronica's. For a second, disappointment and doubt loomed over me because the guilt was too much for me to handle but she smiled up at me and the guilt faded.

Her body fit perfectly beneath mine as she wrapped her legs around my hips and squeezed, pulling me in deeper. Grabbing her wrists, I bound them above her head with one of my hands, pressing them into the mattress. She moaned, pleasure emanating from her with each thrust.

Kailyn ignited a spark deep within me, a confidence I thought I'd never feel again.

"Korbin...please...don't...stop." She arched her back.

She was close to losing it, and so was I.

I thrust into her over and over until her entire body tightened around me and she trembled with her release.

"Korbin!" She dug her nails into my arms, and that was all it took to send me over the edge right along with her.

A moment later, I collapsed onto the bed beside her and stared up at the ceiling. I was more confused than ever. I'd just had sex for the first time since my wife died, and it was mind-blowing, but why did I still feel this guilt in the pit of my stomach? Emotion caught in the back of my throat, but I pushed down my feelings so I could concentrate on Kailyn. It wasn't fair to her to just get up and walk away. I needed to keep my emotions in check until I could get away.

I looked over at her. She laid beside me with an intoxicating grin on her face, and I surprisingly smiled back at her without even thinking. It was a normal reaction to her, and I couldn't stop it. I didn't want to.

"Are you okay?" Clearly she was. Or at least she seemed to be.

She flashed another euphoric grin. "I'm more than okay. You're incredible." She turned onto her side and hugged an arm across my chest.

Her eyes narrowed slightly. "Are you okay?"

I stared back up at the ceiling, because I knew I was going to lie to her. "Yeah. I'm good." I cut my eyes toward the door across the room. "Listen, we have to get up early in the morning. I'm going to go get ready for bed."

I slid out from under her grasp and stood to put my shorts back on. Blowing out a breath, I squeezed my eyes shut for a moment then turned to face her.

Leaning over the bed, I gave her a quick kiss. "Goodnight."

Her eyes widened and her mouth opened slightly. She didn't respond, just pulled the sheet up to her chest. As I realized what an asshole I was being to her, I walked away and left her there alone. Once in my own room, I closed the door and leaned my back against the sturdy wood.

Veronica's photo still hung on the wall above the bed… our bed. Her bright smile and playful gaze shone down on me through the pastel canvas and guilt hit me, again, like a punch in the stomach.

Bending over, I put my hands on my knees and exhaled. "God, Veronica. I'm sorry."

Gathering myself enough to move, I walked to the master bath to take a hot shower and try to make sense of what had just happened. While in the shower, anger continued to build as I replayed the night Veronica died as well as what had happened with Kailyn just moments ago.

"What have I done?" I mumbled to myself. "Ahhh! Dammit!" I picked up a bottle of shampoo and slung it across the shower. It hit the wall and the top popped off, splattering the thick liquid against the tile. It washed away as the water pounded against the shower floor. "What have I done?"

Chapter Ten

Kailyn

MY ALARM BLARED THROUGH the early morning darkness, reminding me of how little sleep I'd gotten last night. Rolling out of bed, I flicked the lamp on and squinted to shield my eyes. After I dressed, I made my way down stairs. The smell of coffee and hazelnut filled my nose, making my mouth water.

In the kitchen, Korbin sat at the table reading the newspaper.

"Good morning." I hoped things wouldn't be as awkward between us as they were last night.

Feeling rejected by someone is a horrible feeling, and although I knew what he was going through, I was going through it, too, just in a different way. His feelings mattered, so why didn't mine?

He looked up at me and placed the newspaper down in front of him. "Good morning," he said nonchalantly as if everything was okay.

I nodded and turned to pour myself a cup of coffee—not quite sure how to act around him, then I grabbed the eggs and bacon out of the refrigerator.

"Would you like something to eat?" I broke the awkward silence.

He stood from the table and walked toward the front door. "No, it's okay. I have to go practice." He grabbed his hat off the hook by the front door and positioned it on his head, tipping it just enough so the brim barely covered his eyes. "The rodeo's comin' up, and I need to get my head back in it."

Bacon sizzled in the pan as I flipped each piece. "Okay. I hope you have a good day." I glanced at him over my shoulder.

His lips formed into a tight line, and his jaw tensed. "Kailyn…" he started. "About last night…"

I wasn't about to relive the embarrassment again. Living it all last night was exhausting enough, so I cut him off and ripped the band aid off myself. "It's okay, Korbin. I understand. Your wife passed away, and you feel guilty for having sex with me. I get it," I blurted, placing the last piece of bacon on my plate.

Saying that probably wasn't the best idea, but I wanted him to know I understood his reservations about us, even though it didn't change *my* feelings toward *him*. There was no doubt in my mind I was falling for him, quickly, but I had to hold back for his sake.

His eyes hardened. "She didn't *pass away*," he protested. "She was killed."

The fury in his eyes sent chills down my spine, and I immediately regretted what I'd said.

He took a step back and glanced down. "I'm sorry. I

didn't mean to be so harsh. It's just…it's all so overwhelming and complicated. Plus, I love having you here, and I don't want to lose you." He cleared his throat and quickly added, "As an employee." He rubbed the back of his neck nervously. "I don't want to lose you as the ranch manager."

Okay. I get the point.

Picking my coffee up, I wrapped my hands around the warm cup and turned to gaze out of the kitchen window. "Okay." I shrugged.

I didn't have the right to be bitter, but I was. I was jealous of his dead wife. *Seriously who feels this way?* A horrible person, that's who.

Korbin startled me as he placed both of his hands on my shoulders and ran them down my arms. "Last night was incredible. I mean that, Kailyn." I remained facing the window, my back to him, and closed my eyes. "Please don't think I regret anything about us, because I don't." He leaned in closer. "I'm going to find a way to get through this. It's just an adjustment for me and Kadence." He kissed the back of my head lightly. "Please be patient," he whispered against my hair, then he turned to leave.

Before walking out the front door, he stopped but never turned around. "If this is all too much for you, I would understand if you choose to leave, but I hope you don't." With that, he walked out the door and headed to the barn.

The rest of the day had gone by quickly. After breakfast, I locked myself in my office and hadn't emerged until late afternoon, working hard to learn the ins and outs of how to run the ranch. There was payroll, livestock and crop sales, rodeo earnings, and other expenses I knew very little about. Although I loved numbers, it was enough to make anyone's head spin.

My saving grace had been an organized binder Veronica had kept with detailed instructions for how to run the ranch. It included everything from championship and crop earnings information to employees' salaries and other expenses. I'd never been more thankful to have a college degree and this dusty, black binder than I was now. As I walked outside of the barn to get some sunshine, a yellow school bus came up the long drive.

Oh, crap. Kadence. I'm responsible for her, too. Not just the farm. Korbin had forgotten to mention when she'd be back home.

It was late summer and school had just started back. She stepped off the bus with a pink camo backpack slung over her shoulder. Her long, dark hair was up in a ponytail and about the same length as her mom's, from what I'd seen in photos.

As she got closer, I stood there contemplating what I was going to say to her, but her eyes were wet and swollen as if she'd been crying. She quickly dropped her head and ran past me and into the house.

Should I go after her or just leave her alone?

Scanning the property, I couldn't see Korbin anywhere, so I decided to go check on her.

The sound of little sobs drifted down the hallway as I walked up the stairs and rounded the corner to her room.

I knocked lightly on the door. "Kadence?" I slowly pushed the door open enough to see in. "It's me, Kailyn. I'd like to come in and talk if that's okay?" I asked cautiously, not sure how to approach the situation exactly. I was just winging it.

"Go away," she cried.

"Are you sure?" I started to pull back, but decided to try one more time. "I can come in and just listen if you'd like to talk about it." I waited for a moment and when she didn't answer, I walked further into the room. She wiped her nose with her arm, and when she didn't yell for me to leave I sat on the edge of the bed beside of her. "What's wrong, sweetie?"

She pulled her knees to her chest. "Nothing," she snapped.

This isn't going to be easy...

KORBIN

I hadn't heard Kadence's school bus arrive, but I knew it was time for her to get home, so I walked inside to see if she was in yet. Standing in the hallway, I peeked through the crack in the door and watched Kailyn and Kadence together. I froze. Watching them was bittersweet. Part of me enjoyed seeing her interacting with a woman again, but the other part of me didn't because Veronica should be there talking to her. I fought the urge to bust in on them and find out why Kadence was crying, but I waited and watched because it was important to me to see how Kailyn handled whatever was going on.

"It's okay. I know you don't know me that well, but you can trust me." Her voice was gentle as she spoke. She put a hand on Kadence's arm. "If you ever need to talk about anything, I'm here. No matter what it is."

Kadence raised her head and looked at Kailyn, tears streaming down her face. I wanted to know what was wrong with my baby girl. What had made her so upset? But once again…I waited. Something told me to wait.

"It's a boy in my class," Kadence said between sniffles.

Kailyn scowled. "Did this boy hurt you?"

That a girl, Kailyn.

"No. Well…kinda." She paused and her lip trembled. "He called me ugly and said my momma died because she didn't love me anymore."

Her eyes were red and swollen, and my heart broke into a million pieces for her.

I'd never wanted to bring violence upon a child before, but I was considering it after that confession from Kadence. How could any child say something so hurtful? I wanted to run in and hug Kadence, protect her, but I was too choked up and angry by how hurt she was.

Anger flashed across Kailyn's face, but she quickly reeled it in enough to try calming Kadence down.

She tucked a strand of hair behind Kadence's ear. "Honey, listen. First, this boy has no idea what he's talking about. Your mom loved you with all of her heart, and she died because of a tragic accident, not because she didn't love you." She grabbed Kadence by the hand and led her to the mirror hanging above her dresser. "Second, now, look. Nothing about you is ugly, Kadence. You're beautiful. You look just like your mother."

I stepped back and almost lost my balance, leaning against the door frame for support.

"Really?" Kadence asked, with a half-smile.

Kailyn smiled and placed her arms on Kadence's

shoulders. "Yes, really. You have her shiny, dark hair, her honey-brown eyes, and her smile."

Kadence smiled at herself in the mirror. A little bigger and brighter this time.

"See. That's it. That smile right there." Kailyn bent down and squinted toward the mirror. "Wait. What's that?"

"What's what?" Kadence touched her face.

"Those," Kailyn said, touching the dimples on Kadence's cheeks, and then the one on her chin. "Okay, nevermind. You look exactly like your mother *except* for those cute dimples you have." She stood upright again and nodded toward the mirror, matter-of-factly. "Yep, those dimples are definitely your father's." She laughed.

Kadence giggled and smiled again, poking her fingers into her dimples. "Yeah, I guess you're right."

Kailyn's face grew serious, and she turned Kadence to face her. "I don't know why that stupid boy said what he did, but I know without a doubt your mom is looking down on you, and she's so proud of you and your daddy." She placed her palm over Kadence's heart. "A piece of her will always live with you, in here."

Just when I thought the crying was over, Kadence's chin trembled and tears filled her eyes once again. She sobbed. "I miss her so much."

Tears filled my own eyes as I watched her. I hated seeing my daughter in so much pain, knowing I couldn't do any-thing to take that pain away.

Kailyn pulled Kadence against her into a hug and rubbed her head. "I know you do, sweetie. I'm so sorry. It's not fair." She inhaled deeply and looked up at the ceiling, trying to stop herself from crying.

For someone who didn't have any children, Kailyn sure was handling this like she had a lot of experience with them. It was refreshing to see Kadence confide in Kailyn—to have an outlet besides me. Maybe she needed a woman's touch to get her through this.

Kadence's sobs lessened, and she pulled away from Kailyn. "Thank you, Kailyn." She sniffled. "I feel better now."

"Good." Kailyn smiled. "I'm just down the hall if you ever need me. My door is always open to you, okay?" She rubbed her head.

Kadence sat on the bed, grabbed a nearby pillow and hugged it to her chest. "Okay."

Quietly, I hurried down the hall to my room, trying to figure out how I felt about what had just happened. I was thankful for Kailyn being there for Kadence, but it hurt to see another woman consoling my daughter.

A quiet knock broke me from my thoughts. I opened the door and Kailyn pushed past me.

She paced back and forth beside my bed. "Look, Korbin. I just realized something, and I need to tell you. I need you to listen. I mean really listen to what I have to say." She took a breath and looked up at me with determination. "Veronica loved you. I know she did. I mean, how could she not?" She shrugged then continued on in a rush, "I understand you're heartbroken and still grieving, and I'm sorry if what happened last night added extra confusion to your life, but I'm not sorry it happened. We're both adults, and we're only human."

She stepped closer to me, her gaze radiating confidence and clarity.

I opened my mouth to speak, but she raised her finger in

protest. "Hang on. Please let me get this all out," she pleaded. "I loved everything about last night and wouldn't change any of it for a second." She swallowed hard. "I'll distance myself if that's what you need. But I want you to know I think we could be really great together if you'd give us a chance."

Her words took my breath away, and every part of my body and soul wanted to reach out to her, take her in my arms, and tell her I wanted the same things. But why did I keep holding back?

I blinked at her and sat down on the oversized chair in the corner of the room.

She continued, "As we both know, Korbin, life is too short to not tell someone how you feel, so this is me telling you how I feel." She threw her arms out by her side. "I'm here, Korbin. Right here. I'm all in when you're ready."

My jaw tensed, and I held back the urge to grab her and kiss her. Between what she was confessing to me, and what I'd just witnessed with her and Kadence, I knew I wanted Kailyn in my life.

She moved in closer. "I want to get to know you better. I want to have more nights like last night. Does that make me selfish? Maybe. But I can't help how I feel." She bent down and rested her hand on my knee. "My heart knows what it wants." She searched my eyes. "Look me in the eyes and tell me you don't feel the same way."

She was right. I did feel the same way. It was fast, but the constant pull between us was strong. Still, I couldn't say it. Not yet.

Her eyes narrowed. "That's what I thought." She stood and took a step back. "Veronica wouldn't want you to torture yourself like this, Korbin, and you know it. She'd want you and Kadence to both be happy. She wouldn't want you to constantly walk around with guilt and pain in your heart." She turned to walk back toward the door but stopped and looked at me over her shoulder. "When you're ready, I'll be here." Then she walked out, closing the door behind her, leaving me stunned silent.

I exhaled a breath I hadn't realized I'd been holding. *Damn.* I did feel the same way about Kailyn, but once I said the words, I knew there'd be no turning back, and that scared the hell out of me, but excited me at the same time. I had to make my mind up, quickly, because it wasn't fair to her.

Chapter Eleven

Kailyn

MY THOUGHTS WERE SCATTERED all over the place as I walked back to my office in the barn. I inhaled a deep, calming breath and admired the scenery around me. Mountains in the distance, reaching as far as my eyes could see, rows of crops lining the property, and the large, red barn in front of me.

I couldn't get Korbin's face out of my mind, or the conversation I'd just had with Kadence in her room. My conversation with Kadence was so easy, and I couldn't understand why. All I know is I talked from the heart and told the truth. Why was I so invested in them both so quickly? Why did I feel the urge to help them? Why couldn't I just walk away, do my job, and leave them alone? I was there to work, not fall in love.

Snowflake, *the forbidden horse*, neighed as I walked by his stall, making me jump. "What is it, boy?"

He reared back onto his hind legs then hung his head over the stall door, shaking his head and snorting at me, making me flinch. If I hadn't known any better, I would've thought he wanted me to pet him. I knew better, though. Korbin would be way too angry. Besides, I knew very little about horses, but I was curious and really wanted to pet him.

"I can't. I'm sorry." I sighed, continuing to my office, leaving him behind.

After a couple of hours of being up to my eyeballs in financial reports, a giggle carried through the barn outside of my door.

I need a break anyway.

Making my way down the small hallway, I turned the corner and stopped. Kadence chased baby pigs in their pens and laughed each time she'd catch one. Without notice, a small laugh bubbled up as I watched her. She was happy, not crying like earlier. It was nice to see. I folded my arms across my chest and leaned against the stall watching her.

She saw me and jumped. "I'm sorry, Kailyn. I hope I'm not being too loud."

"Oh, no," I quickly said. "You go ahead and have fun. I needed a break anyway. Sometimes numbers make my head hurt."

"Mine, too." She giggled. "Hey!" She pepped up. "Do you wanna go horseback riding with me?" Her eyes widened and she bounced up and down.

I laughed apprehensively. "I don't know. I don't think that's such a great idea. I've never been on a horse before," I admitted, but riding a horse was on my bucket list.

She dropped her head and sulked out of the pig pen, looking disappointed. "Okay."

This girl was good. No wonder she had Korbin wrapped around her finger. She was impossible to say no to.

I sighed. "Okay..."

She looked up at me curiously, excitement in her wide eyes as she clapped her hands together and nodded. "Okay? Yes?"

I inhaled deeply then exhaled slowly. "It looks like we're going horseback riding," I agreed. "But, we need to ask your dad first."

She grinned. "Okay."

Her smile was contagious. Even though I was nervous, I couldn't help but smile with her. I had to do this. For her. I couldn't explain the connection between us, but I knew a part of me wanted to see her happy and be there for her.

"What're you doing?" Korbin said, watching us from the doorway of the barn.

His eyes were soft and needing as he looked at me.

Kadence ran over to him. "Taking Kailyn on a ride, Dad! Will you come, too? Please?" She worked her magic on him with her puppy dog eyes.

She was smart, though. I mean, how can anyone say no to that face?

He raised an eyebrow at me. "Have you ever even been on a horse before?"

"No, but I'll be fine," I said, shaking my hands to calm my nerves. "How hard can it be?" I shrugged.

He chuckled and Kadence laughed. "This is gonna be fun."

"I heard that." I made my way over to them. "I'm standing right here ya know."

He walked over to the stalls to get the horses and saddled

them. "I guess I better come along to chaperone."

After each of the horses were saddled and ready, Kadence introduced me to them. She grabbed the reins of the smaller, black horse. "Kailyn, this is my horse, Midnight." She kissed him on the single white spot on his snout, then she walked over to the next horse. "This horse is, Champion. He's dad's horse." She continued to the next one. "This is your horse. His name is Spot." She patted him on the neck. He was white with gray spots, which is where I'm guessing he got his name. "He's very old and gentle, so he's a good one for beginners."

I laughed. "Well, thank you for giving me the gentle one."

She stepped on a stool by Midnight, placed her left foot in the stirrup, and threw her other leg around to mount the horse.

Easy enough.

Korbin stepped over to my horse, Spot. "Need help?" He grinned.

I tried to hide my fear and boost my own confidence. "No, thanks. I've got it. Have a little faith."

Putting my foot in the stirrup, I tried pulling myself up onto the horse, but it was harder than it looked. I failed, miserably, and slid back down with a grunt. Korbin and Kadence both snickered at my expense.

I looked up at Kadence curiously. "How did you get up there?" I scowled. "You made it look so easy."

She giggled and looked down at me. "That's because it is easy." She pointed at the stirrup. "Just put your foot there, and use your hands and leg to pull and push yourself up at the same time, then swing the other leg over. Easy peasy." She snapped the buckle of her pink-trimmed helmet under her chin. "I'll meet y'all outside. Hurry!" She galloped off on

Midnight.

Easy peasy my....

"You sure you don't want any help?" Korbin smirked.

He only fueled my desire to prove I could do it myself. "I'm sure."

Putting my foot in the stirrup, I gripped the saddle, grunting loudly as I tried pulling myself up. I failed once again. The horse was so tall...

Korbin approached me from behind. "Here. Like this." He put one hand on my leg and moved the stirrup so that it was on the ball of my foot. "You're trying to push yourself up with the tips of your toes. Try it again."

He placed his other hand on the back of my thigh. I glanced at him over my shoulder—his face inches from mine. My body responded to his touch, and I fell back into him slightly.

He cleared his throat. "Okay, on the count of three push up with the foot that's in the stirrup, and I'll help throw your other leg over."

I nodded. "Okay."

His lips were dangerously close to mine as he spoke, "One. Two. Three." He pushed me up in one swift motion, making me yelp as I landed on the horse's back.

I grabbed franticly at the reins. "Thank you." I was absolutely terrified, but I didn't want to admit it.

He nodded and tipped his cowboy hat, then he gracefully got onto his horse with very little effort.

Show off.

When he reached the doorway, he stopped. "Are you coming?"

My horse just stood there. "How do you make this thing

go?"

Korbin shook his head and laughed. I mean genuinely laughed. It was a mesmerizing sound. "Give his sides a little squeeze with your heels and a 'click click' with your tongue," he prompted, demonstrating the 'click click'.

I did what he said, and Spot moved forward. "I did it! He's moving!" I laughed. "Whoa now." He began to trot, bouncing me around uncomfortably as we made our way out of the barn. "Not too fast."

Korbin let me ride in the fenced-in ring, and he and Kadence both helped me learn how to control Spot and feel comfortable on him.

Once Spot began trotting again, I leaned back, pulling on the reins to stop him. "Whoa." I pulled a little harder, coming to a stop beside Kadence.

"We really have to work on your form." She giggled. "You look like a sack of potatoes up there."

Korbin covered his mouth and chuckled.

"Hey. Be gentle will ya?" I laughed. "This is my first time on a horse you know."

Once I finally got the hang of how to safely and correctly *operate* a horse without looking like a *sack of potatoes*, we were on our way to explore the farm.

"For your first time, you're doing pretty good!" Kadence giggled. "Better than we thought you would." She shrugged.

Korbin and Kadence rode ahead of me to a nearby trail and talked and laughed together. It was comforting seeing Korbin interact with her. She brought out his softer carefree side, and I loved seeing it.

It was almost nightfall, so after a brief ride through the woods, we returned to the barn. After securing the horses in their stalls, Korbin walked around the corner to check on some of the other animals before going in for dinner.

Kadence closed the stall door and locked it. "I had so much fun with you today." She smiled up at me. "I'm really glad you're here." She turned to walk away, but stopped for a moment once she reached the door. Turning to face me, she said, "He may not admit it yet, but my dad is really glad you're here, too." She turned and walked back to the house to wash up for dinner.

The thought of Korbin actually being glad I was there made me smile.

I'm glad I'm here, too.

With each passing day, I began to see myself having a future here.

In the kitchen, I gathered what I needed to make dinner. Kadence walked in wearing bright pink pajamas, and her hair was still wet from her bath.

"Can I help?"

"Of course." I touched my flour covered finger to her nose.

She laughed and stepped up on a nearby stool. "What're you cooking?"

"*We're* making a homemade pizza." I bent down as if I had some huge secret and whispered, "It's my grandma's secret recipe."

Making pizza with my grandma was one of the last memories I had of her. Before she fell ill, I used to go stay with her on weekends for pizza and movie nights. She was the only constant in my life, until she passed away. She probably saw me more than my own parents.

I continued, "I'll share the recipe with you, but you have to promise not to say anything to anyone—not even your dad." I extended my pinky to her.

Her eyes lit up with excitement. "I promise." She linked her pinky with mine. "Pinky promise."

We laughed and continued gathering ingredients for our pizza. "Hang on a second." I grabbed my phone. "We need some music." I connected my phone to the same speaker system I'd used earlier with Korbin. "Let me introduce you to what my best friend and I always do when we're cooking together."

KORBIN

My body and hands ached from working on the farm all day. I really shouldn't have gone on the ride with Kadence, but I knew it was important to her.

Building new stalls and filling up troughs for rescues that were going to be delivered soon, fixing a half mile worth of fence around the property line, and harvesting crops and preparing them to be shipped out to local grocery stores was only the tip of the iceberg.

Walking into the house, I kicked my boots off and hung my cowboy hat on the hook by the door. The smell of garlic was so strong it tickled my nose, almost making me sneeze, and the sound of music filled the entire house as I walked toward the kitchen.

Kailyn. I sighed.

You'd think there was a house party going on. "Josh Turner?" I mumbled.

Go figure. Even the city girl knows who Josh Turner is. His deep voice puts the rest of us to shame.

Peeking around the corner, I watched Kadence and Kailyn dance around the kitchen, using spatulas as microphones. Kadence threw her head back and twirled, laughing. It had been a while since I'd heard her belly laugh like that.

Emotion caught in my throat as I looked on silently. They both rocked back and forth in front of each other as they took turns singing. I chuckled. Kailyn was so good with her. Kadence hadn't taken up with anyone since her mother passed away, so it was refreshing to see her out of her bedroom, laughing instead of crying.

Taking a moment to gather myself, I turned to a photo of Veronica on the wall. "I wish you could see this. See her. She's smiling and laughing again. She seems more like our little firecracker." I knew she couldn't hear me, but talking to her anyway sometimes helped. "We miss you so much." I rubbed the back of my head and stepped closer to the photo. "But the good news is she's healing, and so am I. We're going to be okay."

Inhaling deeply, I peeked back around the corner. Kailyn spun around and reached out to touch Kadence's cheek, leaving a white streak of flour behind. Kadence laughed then grabbed some flour and jumped up to put it on Kailyn's nose. Kailyn's eyes widened then she chased Kadence around the kitchen with flour all over her hands. Kadence ran around the kitchen island, until Kailyn finally caught her and smeared flour across her face.

My kitchen was wrecked, and flour was everywhere, but I couldn't stop them because it was somewhat comforting to watch. Watching them gave me an idea. I wanted to join in on the fun.

Sneaking off, I walked into the garage to get my own toy then returned to the kitchen.

"What's going on in here?" I startled them, making them both freeze.

Kailyn's eyes locked with mine, and the playfulness in her gaze dimmed slightly, as if she thought she was in trouble.

Kadence walked back over to the mixing bowl. "Just cooking dinner." She continued kneading the dough on the counter.

"Sure you are." I chuckled.

Grinning roguishly, I pulled a water gun from behind my back. Both of them looked at me, their mouths wide open.

Kailyn's eyes narrowed. "You wouldn't."

I glanced down at the gun then back at her. "Oh, but I would, darlin'."

Kadence was the first to squeal, then Kailyn joined in as I started squirting them. In the moment, it was like we were a family. Yes, it was quick, and guilt snagged me a bit, but it felt natural and just...*right*. Clean-up was going to be *a lot* of fun, but that's okay. I'd do anything to see my baby girl happy again.

After dinner, Kadence headed upstairs to once again get cleaned up and ready for bed.

Kailyn and I followed shortly behind and walked into her room to tell her goodnight.

She relaxed into her pillow and cuddled her white, stuffed horse. "Thank you for today, Kailyn." She yawned, struggling to keep her heavy eyelids open. "It was a lot of fun."

"It's really easy to have fun with you." Kailyn smiled. "I'm sorry the pizza didn't turn out as great as usual." She laughed. "I think we went a little overboard on the flour."

"It's okay. The best part was making it with you." Kadence yawned once more before closing her eyes.

Kailyn placed her hand over her heart, and tears glistened in her eyes.

Kadence and Veronica used to cook dinner together all the time. It was a special memory they'd shared, and now, I had to make the decision of whether or not I was okay with her making special memories with someone else. The woman I was rapidly falling for.

Kailyn

We stood in the hallway outside Kadence's room. Korbin wrapped his arms around me. "You're so good with her," he whispered. "Thank you."

I snuggled into his chest. "You don't have to thank me. She's a great little girl."

He pulled back and grinned. "I'm gonna call the sitter and have her come watch Kadence." His grin spread wider into a genuine smile. "I want to take you somewhere."

"Okay." I laughed. "Where?"

He pulled his phone out of his pocket and dialed who I assumed was the babysitter. "Go get your dress and cowboy boots on." He brought his phone up to his ear.

"What? Why?"

He twisted the phone away from his mouth and said, "We're goin' dancin'."

I raised an eyebrow. "Oh, no. Nope." I shook my head. "No, thank you. I don't line dance."

I could picture it now...*Hee-hawing* and *Boot Scootin' Boogieing* straight to the floor as I trip over my own feet. No way.

He gave me an amused look. "See you downstairs in an hour."

Groaning, I forced myself to go get ready. He's already gotten me up on a mechanical bull and somehow taught me how to ride a horse. I shrugged. So, what's one more thing to add to the list? How hard can line dancing really be anyway?

It was nearing ten thirty when Korbin knocked. "Let's go, or we're gonna be late," he called through the door. "Babysitter is here, so just meet me downstairs."

I walked down the stairs with my boots in my hand. "I'm coming. Sheesh. Impatient much?"

Korbin looked up at me with wide eyes, and his jaw tensed.

"What's wrong?" Looking down, I fluffed my knee-length, red dress with my other hand. "I knew I shouldn't have worn this dress."

He blinked up at me. "No. It's perfect." He smiled. "You look great."

I finished my descent and bent over to put my boots on at the bottom of the stairs. "I still can't believe I've traded in my heels for boots." I laughed.

"Boots look good on you," he said, making me blush. The tone in his voice made me feel special.

I curtsied. "Thank you, sir." I grabbed his arm. "Now, let's go before I change my mind."

We arrived at the bar, and I stopped in my tracks as I spotted the dancers on the dance floor. "No way." I shook my head. "I can't do that. Nuh-uh."

There were what looked to be about ten couples on the large dance floor. I watched as a man spun his partner around in a million different directions then passed her on to someone else. Just watching them made me dizzy. Their feet moved in ways I'd never seen before. Kicking one way, scooting the other, grape vining one way and then some other move I'd never even seen before. I was way out of my comfort zone. There was no way I could do that kind of dancing.

"Relax." He coaxed me with his eyes. "Most of these people are seasoned line dancers. Not all of the dances are like *that*, or that complicated."

We found a table and ordered our drinks. I bounced

my leg nervously under the table as I continued to watch the dancers.

With each changing song, I studied the moves and tried to remember them. Korbin leaned in and explained to me what each move was called from the box step to the pin-wheel, and everything in between.

"Don't be nervous." Korbin placed his hand on my thigh. "This is supposed to be fun."

The band ended the current song, and the lead singer spoke into the mic. "We're gonna slow it down a bit for all you lovers out there." He took a moment to tune his guitar to prepare for the change of song. "How about a little Ronan Keating, *When You Say Nothing at All*?"

He counted off the band, and the lights above the dance floor dimmed to a majestic blue as they began playing.

Korbin stood from the table and pulled his hat off, touching it to his chest. He extended his hand. "Ms. North, there's only one way to get over your fear." A sly grin spread across his lips, and my heart melted all over again. "May I have this dance?"

I glanced at the dance floor then back at him. "Okay. I can handle slow dancing." I took his hand.

He led me through the crowd to a spot near the corner of the stage. It was darker than the rest of the dance floor, so I felt more comfortable there. I was pretty sure he did that on purpose, to help calm my nerves.

I wrapped my arms around his neck and searched his eyes. The lead singer crooned into the microphone, his baritone voice singing about how a person says it best when they say nothing at all. The song made perfect sense while looking deeply into Korbin's eyes. Even through the darkness, I felt his eyes on me.

I'd always heard people say the eyes are windows to a person's soul, and this moment with Korbin made me a believer. Neither of us said anything. We didn't have to. Both of us drank the other in—getting lost in each other's gaze. It was an intense moment for me. He was looking past all of my insecurities, straight to my soul.

As we swayed together to the music, all of my nerves disappeared, and I'd forgotten anyone else was around. It was just us. We were all that mattered, and I didn't want the moment to end. If I could relive this moment with Korbin, I would a million times.

Korbin leaned in, his face inches from mine. After a second, he tenderly placed a kiss on my lips, lingering for a few seconds which I adored. He pulled away then tugged me gently against his chest, wrapping his arms tighter around my back.

Closing my eyes, I concentrated on the music, enjoying the last few moments of being wrapped in Korbin's arms. Out of all the lyrics in the song, there was one line I couldn't get out of my head. The singer sang about how nothing could define what's being said between their hearts. That one line fit us perfectly. Korbin and I may have been falling in love too quickly for some to understand, but that's okay because we understood each other, and that's all that mattered.

The song ended, making me frown. "Okay, lovebirds," the lead singer announced. "Time to take it back up a notch."

Being from the city, I hadn't grown up listening to a lot of country music. Okay, barely any, but I'd done my research since meeting Korbin. Tracy Lawrence was one of Korbin's favorite singers, so I recognized the song *Alibis* as the band began to play.

Just as I started to bolt back to my seat, he tightened his grip on my hand and pulled me back to him. "Come on," he pleaded. "One more."

As couples gathered around, I hesitated. "This isn't just a line dance. It's a couple's line dance." I tried to swallow my nerves. "Those are much harder, Korbin."

"It's okay." He gestured to a corner of the dance floor. "We'll practice over here for a moment before joining the group."

He wrapped one arm around my back. "Put your left hand up on my shoulder," he instructed. I did as he said. "Great. Now, put your other hand in mine and bend your elbow."

Butterflies fluttered in my stomach. Experiencing new things with Korbin was exhilarating. It was hard to describe, but I wanted to do these things for him. With him. I wanted to take chances and challenge myself to try new things. I wanted to be in his life, and I wanted this to be *our* life. I wanted to explore everything possible with this man.

"Now." He looked down at our feet. "It starts with the box step. Step back with your right foot when I say one. Then step left with your left foot, up with your left foot, then right with your right foot. A box." He smiled. "Simple."

"Simple," I echoed nervously. "Right…"

Just like riding a horse was supposed to be 'easy peasy'. This is going to be a disaster.

He leaned in so his cheek was against mine, his lips grazing my ear as he whispered, "One, two, three, one, two three." He counted as I tried to remember to make a box with my feet.

His breath tickled my skin, making me shiver, and I closed my eyes and got lost in his voice. Inhaling deeply, I breathed in his cologne, savoring the smell of him. So manly and sexy.

I'd gotten a little too lost in the music and stepped on his foot. I jumped back slightly. "Oops." My cheeks warmed with embarrassment.

"It's okay." He grinned. "Let's try again, while turning this time."

He must have lost his mind. I'd just stepped on him during an easy box step, and now he wanted to add trickery into the mix.

I exhaled and resumed the correct form. "Just feel the music and let me lead you," he reminded. Before I knew it, I was doing the steps while turning in different directions.

KORBIN

No matter what challenge I'd thrown at Kailyn, she'd always at least tried whatever it was, and so far, she'd been surprisingly great at everything. Her audaciousness made me fall for her even more. She was a venturesome woman, and I loved that about her.

"Come on. You're ready." I led Kailyn toward the circle.

She sighed. "Why do I let you talk me into things like this?"

I smirked. "Because they're fun?"

She rolled her eyes, playfully. "Let's do this before I change my mind and run."

As we made our way to join the crowd, Julia, Veronica's

best friend, looked at Kailyn then back at me. She shook her head and frowned. The last time I'd gone dancing like this was with Veronica. I'd been so eager to take Kailyn out I'd forgotten at some point I'd have to face everyone with the reality that I'd eventually have to move on with my life.

It wasn't going to be easy because everyone knew and loved Veronica. The guilt I'd worked hard to push out of my mind reared its head again after seeing the disappointment on Julia's face, but I pushed through it and concentrated on Kailyn. I'd have to deal with everyone else later. Tonight was about her.

We quickly slipped in between two couples and danced clockwise with the group. Kailyn studied the couple in front of us with such intensity—watching every move. She mimicked their movements and had a few missteps, but I pretended not to notice. Her face flushed as she almost tripped over her own feet, and her nervousness returned, but she continued to try.

One, two, three, one, two, three, I counted out loud, explaining to Kailyn each step as it happened. She was still a little overwhelmed, but after a few rounds she started to loosen up and enjoy herself.

After doing the pinwheel, I pulled her into a wrap. She fit perfectly under my arm.

I could get used to this…

We continued to waltz forward with the group. I glanced over and smiled. After another pinwheel, I pulled her back into another wrap, and she lost her balance, almost falling. To my surprise, she laughed, and her voice carried through the crowd of people around us. It reached deep inside me, and the hardened shell around my heart was crumbling, fast.

As scary as it was to see how quickly she'd been able to disarm me and my reservations, I was glad she had because I'd lost myself in a sea of darkness over the past year, but with Kailyn, I was beginning to find myself again. Find my light again.

"This is so much fun. I can't believe I'm country line dancing." She laughed. "I'll be a pro before you know it."

"You're doing a fine job." I grinned. "Just don't trade in the heels for cowgirl boots, just yet…"

"Hey now." She nudged me with her shoulder. "Thank you for pushing me out of my comfort zone. I could get used to this." She smiled.

I twirled her around and pulled her tight against my chest, whispering in her ear. "Honey, you ain't seen nothin' yet. Just wait. I have other things I can't wait to show you."

She shivered as she leaned against me. She stiffened and pressed her thighs together, and I couldn't help but groan, knowing she'd reacted that way because her body ached to feel me again.

She blushed. "I'm glad you're amused."

She bit her lip and smiled up at me, raising an eyebrow seductively.

Leaning down, I whispered against her ear, "If you bite your lip like that again, I'm gonna have to show you those things a little sooner than anticipated."

"Oh, really?" she teased. "Promise?"

I winked. "You bet."

After hours of dancing, I was exhausted, but I couldn't re-member the last time I'd smiled this much in one night. As I laid in bed, I let out a sigh, thinking about how quickly my life had changed. All because of Kailyn. No woman, besides Veronica, had ever been able to catch my attention like she has and move me the ways she'd moved me. I couldn't ex-plain it. No matter how much I fought it, I couldn't resist her. I could physically feel myself being drawn to her. Things between us were happening so quickly, and I wasn't sure my mind had caught up with my heart just yet.

When Kailyn was near me, I couldn't help but want to make her happy—see her smile. Thinking back to the day I'd first met her, I remembered watching her and thinking to myself she was a beautiful woman, but she probably wouldn't make it on the ranch. I was wrong. Then again, I'd thought the same about Veronica when I'd first met her, and she, too, surprised me. Hell, I ended up marrying her.

It wasn't fair to compare Kailyn to Veronica, I knew that, but the feelings that were developing between Kailyn and I were very similar, so it was hard not to.

Certain things Kailyn would do, like the way she tilts her head to the side when she laughs, or how easily it was to make her blush, or how she'd bite her lip just before I kissed her. Those were all similarities that were hard to miss. I tossed and turned, unable to sleep. It was going to be a long night.

Sleeping was apparently not going to happen. I couldn't stop thinking about the entire day and night and how much fun

I'd had. Horseback riding, dancing and making dinner with Kadence, Korbin squirting us with water guns, then our dancing at the Honky-Tonk bar.

I smiled as I remembered every detail of the night, but then I frowned.

What was I doing? Why had feelings developed so quickly?

The moon shone through the window, landing delicately on the face of a large clock on the wall. Three in the morning and no doubt Korbin would have me up, working by six. I tossed and turned until I finally got the nerve to go see him. He'd be up soon, anyway, and I knew I wasn't going to be getting any sleep, knowing he's so close.

Padding down the hallway, butterflies filled my stomach as I neared his door. I'd knock one time, and if he didn't answer, I'd have to wait to see him in the morning. I didn't want to wake him, but I really wanted to be with him.

I knocked lightly on his door. "It's three in the morning, Kailyn. What're you doing?" I mumbled to myself. He was probably sleeping. That's what normal people do in the middle of the night. After he didn't answer, I turned and started back toward my room.

I probably seem like a crazy person right now.

After taking a few steps, the door opened behind me, stopping me in my tracks. "Kailyn?" He yawned. "Is something wrong?"

I turned to face him. He stood in the doorway with nothing but his boxer-briefs on. *This is exactly what I want.* The attraction I had toward this man was ridiculously annoying, but very welcomed.

His muscles cast shadows on the wall from the soft glow

of the lamp inside, making me want to reach out and stroke his abs, and trace the cut lines that disappeared beneath the cotton hugging his hips.

I cleared my throat. "Nothing's wrong. That's the problem. Everything is so right. I'm sorry to wake you, but I can't sleep. My mind is racing. I know it's late, but I really want to be with you," I blurted.

"Now?" He glanced over at the clock on the nightstand.

He didn't give me time to respond before stepping back and motioning for me to come inside. He walked over and took a seat on the edge of the bed.

I paced the floor in front of him, finally gathering enough courage to sit beside him.

"Maybe I'm overstepping my boundaries. I mean look what happened with Kadence today, and now I'm here in your bedroom after telling you I would wait, but the truth is I can't get you off my mind, no matter how hard I try."

He blinked at me, seeming more awake and rubbed his hand through his hair. I was happy to see he wasn't about to fall asleep on me.

He rested his forehead against mine for a moment. "Stop talking. Please," he whispered. "You didn't overstep. If anything, I think she needed you today more than she needed me. As hard as it is for me to admit that, I could see she was comfortable talking to you and you helped open her up." He frowned. "She barely talks to me about anything anymore."

"You're doing a great job with her. Don't beat yourself up so badly." I leaned closer and grabbed his hand. "She's a little girl. Sometimes all she needs is a pep talk. That's all," I said reassuringly. "You're a wonderful father, Korbin. Kadence is lucky to have you." I smiled at him, and he grinned back.

"One more thing." I rested my palm on his thigh. "Is it okay that I'm here?"

He chuckled, then grabbed me and kissed me. No warning. He just did it. I melted into his arms as he wrapped one hand around my back and the other around my hair, pulling me toward him. After a moment, he pulled back, breaking the kiss. Slowly, I opened my eyes and brought my fingertips to my lips. I wasn't sure what had just happened, but I liked it.

His eyes softened. "Kailyn, you're one of the most challenging, yet captivating, women I've ever met." He shook his head. "I have no idea what the future holds for us, but I do know one thing. I laughed tonight. I mean really and truly laughed. I haven't laughed like that in way too long. I've been walking around in my own personal hell for over a year, and in such a short time, you've made me feel alive again." He leaned in and caressed my cheek. "I have to figure out how to do this—how to close one chapter of my life and start a new one."

He kissed me again, then pulled me onto his lap. "And, yes, it's okay for you to be here."

I straddled him, my knees bent on the bed, pressing into the mattress.

My body trembled with want, and I needed him to devour me and lose himself in me. I yearned to be the one thing he could hold on to. To be his rock. His reason to move on.

His look was intense, making me shiver. He turned and rolled me onto the bed so that he was on top of me. Then, slowly, he peeled my shorts and shirt off.

Sitting back on his heels at the foot of the bed, he stared at me in awe. Being completely naked usually made me uncomfortable, but the last time Korbin had seen me naked, he'd made me feel beautiful. Scar and all.

He leaned over and kissed the top of my foot, moving his lips up my leg and inner thigh, over my hip and stomach, then his mouth explored one breast while his hand caressed the other.

Closing my eyes, a gentle moan escaped my lips. His strong hands and warm mouth on my body made me crave more. He pulled his underwear off and pushed my legs apart with his knee. His lips met mine again as he entered me. Stretching me. Filling me.

Feeling him, skin to skin, was euphoric. On our way back from line dancing, he'd asked me if I was on birth control, and I'd assured him I was, so I was anxious to see how our next sexual encounter played out.

Sex had never felt so powerful before. Then again, I didn't have a lot to compare it to. I lost my virginity in high school to a boy who I'm pretty sure finished before we'd even gotten started. The only other man I'd been with was Mason, and although he was great in bed, he was never emotionally connected to me like this. He wanted to have rough sex and be done, but Korbin took his time and wanted me to truly feel every part of him.

Our bodies moved in sync as we both let go of everything and just enjoyed each other. This was us moving on. Together.

I looked into his eyes with every thrust. The moonlight shone through the curtains, making his blue eyes shine like glittery stars in the night sky.

Reaching up, I wrapped my hands around his neck, pulling him down to me. He kissed along my neck below my ear. A moan escaped his lips so deeply it shook me to my core.

My body tensed around his, and he thrust harder and faster, hungry with intense passion.

Gripping the crisp, cotton sheet with both hands, I twisted it around my fingers and allowed myself to feel him. *Really* feel him. It was too much to handle. I wanted to scream. I wanted to cry. I wanted release. My body and mind were wound tightly, about to erupt. The emotional connection we shared made me feel like my soul was going to jump right out of my body and straight into his.

He closed the gap between us and captured my lips in another passionate kiss, and after one final thrust, I was done. That was it. My back arched, and I raised my hips to meet his as I found my release, exhaling with pleasure as I squirmed below him, bringing him to his.

Rolling over onto his back, he breathed heavily, rubbing his face with his hand. He sighed deeply and ran his hands through his hair.

Here we go. Will he pull away from me again? He acts so sure about his feelings for me during sex, but now that it's over, will he become a recluse with guilt and uncertainty?

Was I wrong for wanting him to pull me into his arms and hold me? I was trying to be patient with him; I really was, but my heart couldn't take the distance this time.

The silence in the room was agonizing, so I spoke up, "I guess I should go shower and try to get some sleep before the sun comes up." I pulled the sheet against my naked chest and sat on the edge of the bed as I looked for my pajamas.

He sat up behind me, moved my hair to one side and gently kissed my shoulder. "You're amazing, Kailyn North. You know that?" he whispered against my skin.

I glanced at him over my shoulder. "I do now, but you

can tell me again." I grinned, feeling relieved he hadn't pulled away from me again.

He chuckled and kissed me gently. "You're amazing," he repeated.

This. This is what I wanted.

Finally—my clothes. After putting my pajama shirt and shorts back on, I crawled over to him on the bed and kissed him. "Goodnight." I exhaled against his lips. "Sweet dreams."

He kissed me again, and his brows furrowed. "Stay," he whispered.

The shock of his request made me freeze. He needed me. Even if he was struggling to admit it. Him asking me to stay in bed with him was a start.

Without a word, I nodded, slipping back under the covers.

He turned onto his side, away from me. I knew him asking me to stay was a huge step. Just being there, beside of him, was gratifying enough.

Rolling from my back to my side, the soft glow of the full moon lit up the room inviting me to admire him. The white sheet draped delicately over his tanned skin.

Taking a deep breath, I slid closer and nestled my body against his back, wrapping an arm around his waist. He drew in a sharp breath, his body tensing beneath my touch. His reaction caught me off guard, but after a few seconds he relaxed and rested his hand on top of mine. My mind and body relaxed with his as we both drifted off to sleep.

Chapter Twelve

KORBIN

BLINKING THE SLEEP FROM my eyes, I looked at the
clock on the bedside table.

Six-thirty. No way. That can't be right...

Throwing the blanket off, I headed to the bathroom.
I had a rodeo to prepare for, and I'd hoped to have already
been out practicing. On a normal day, I'd be out working by
five-thirty. Training usually took up the majority of my time
during the rodeo season, so between farm work and being a
single dad, it was really hard to concentrate. Another reason
I was glad to have Kailyn to help run the ranch. One less
thing to worry about.

Looking at myself in the mirror, it hit me...*Kailyn.*

I walked out of the bathroom, and there she was—still
in my bed. Her hair spilled over the pillow, her chest rising
steadily with each breath. She looked angelic.

While leaning against the door-frame for support, I

realized the reason I'd overslept was because of her. I hadn't slept that well in months, and I was thankful to have gotten some quality sleep, even if it was for such a short amount of time. Losing control was something I didn't think was going to happen again, but I had to admit Kailyn was in control of my heart now. Not me.

Not wanting to wake her, I returned to the bathroom to shower, got dressed, and then quietly left the room to go train. I grabbed my hat from the hook by the front door and headed to the barn.

As I passed the stalls, Snowflake came over to his door and nudged me with his muzzle. Looking into his big, round eyes, I was reminded why my wife had loved him so much. Opening the stall door, I led him out to the training field behind the barn. "There ya go, boy. Run and have fun."

He galloped through the twilight.

Walking back inside the barn, I saddled my horse. I needed to get my head back in the game before training on the bull. Distractions weren't good for me right now. Or any bull rider as far as that goes. One disconnect from the bull could cost me my life. To clear my mind, I decided to ride to my favorite spot on my property.

Leading Champion through the trails, we reached a large clearing about a mile from the farm. I'd missed most of the sunrise, but the sky was still painted a fiery glow. Nothing like fresh mountain air and a view of the Whitefish Range to relax me and help me navigate through my own mind more clearly.

It was hard for me to understand the feelings I had for Kailyn. I barely knew her, yet I felt like I'd known her my entire life. It was difficult to explain—even to myself. All I knew was, I had to get my head and heart on the same page. Kailyn deserved a man who was confident in knowing what he wanted, not someone who couldn't make up his damn mind.

I nudged Champion, so he would continue walking, and we made our way back to the barn. Kailyn was waiting for me. Her knee-length, cotton dress blew in the wind as she walked toward me. Once she got closer, I could see there were dandelions on it. Kadence's favorite.

"Hey, cowboy." She bit her lip then smiled. "You gonna take me for a ride?"

I grinned. "I thought I already did, ma'am?" I tipped my hat at her. "Or was that not enough?"

She blushed and giggled. "I have a feeling it's never gonna be enough with you."

I winked at her. "Then I must be doing somethin' right."

She laughed. "On that note…I'm gonna get back to work now."

I chuckled and led Champion inside the barn to put him back in his stall. It was time to jump on the bull for a little more practice.

Get back to work. *Yes, let's do that.*

Kailyn

Korbin locked the wooden gate on Champion's stall. When he turned, he noticed me standing in the doorway of my office. My thoughts turned to what it would be like seeing him up on a bull at a competition.

I stepped into the narrow hallway as he started to walk by. "Can I ask you a question?"

He dusted his hands off and wiped them on his jeans. "Sure."

"Why do you ride bulls?" I asked cautiously. "I mean, it's so dangerous."

He looked at me for a moment, passion radiating from him. Just mentioning bull riding changed his demeanor. He took it very seriously.

"You only see it from a spectator's point of view. The audience only sees a wild few moments of chaos." He circled around me and leaned in closer. "A beast thrashing away in pure madness. But what I see…what I feel. Is eight seconds of clarity." He stopped, and his gaze softened. "I learn more about myself as a man, as a father, and as a human being in that eight seconds, than all the other hours in the day."

I swallowed hard, letting his words sink in.

He leaned in, and with deep conviction, he continued, "It's eight seconds of living intensely and knowing I have what it takes to react to anything that gets thrown my way in the ring and life in general." Passion radiated from him, and he swelled with pride. "Not only that, but when I look into the audience and see Kadence with her little arms in the air, cheering me on, I know she's proud of me." He straightened up and took a step back. "*That's* why I'm a bull-rider," he finished abruptly. "Anything else?"

He left me speechless. I wasn't sure how to respond to that. His conviction made me fall for him even more, but a part of me was still scared for him, and for Kadence. She'd already lost her mother and didn't need to lose her father, too.

After a moment, I finally found my voice. "No. I'm good."

"I have to go train for a few hours on the bull before I go get ready for the rodeo." He kissed me on the cheek. "Would you mind going in to check on Kadence?" He looked at his watch. "My mom will be here shortly to pick her up for the weekend. She's gonna skip this rodeo and go to the carnival with them."

I smiled. "Sure," I said, before heading inside.

Korbin hadn't asked me to come to the rodeo. Did he not want me there? Was he just expecting me to go without having to ask? I didn't even know how to get there...

Kadence's laughter carried down the entryway as I entered the house. She was sitting on the living room floor eating Fruity Pebbles while watching SpongeBob in her pajamas. She laughed, again, then took another bite of her cereal.

"Good morning, Kadence." I made my way over to the couch.

She glanced at me briefly, then turned her attention back to the TV. "Good morning," she piped up.

I relaxed on the sofa against the fluffy pillows and laughed along with her.

After SpongeBob was over, she took her dishes to the kitchen.

"Okay, Kadence, we need to go upstairs and make sure you have everything packed up for your grandma's." I turned the TV off. "She'll be here to get you shortly."

She pointed to a small suitcase by the fireplace. "I'm already packed." She giggled.

How old is this kid again? She's so self-sufficient.

"Okay, then." I nodded, making my way over to load the dishwasher.

Looking out the window, I saw Korbin talking to a lady with silver hair. They were standing by what looked like a brand new Cadillac. *That must be his mom.* He pointed at the house and seemed to be annoyed, or a little upset about something as they talked. I wondered if he was telling her about me. About us. I gulped as I thought about having to face his family at some point. Korbin threw his hands out to his sides and shook his head before retreating and coming inside. His mom followed closely behind.

"Nana!" Kadence ran toward the door.

"Hey, sweetheart." She enveloped Kadence in a hug. "Are you ready to go to the carnival tonight?"

Kadence ran over and picked her suitcase up. "I am."

Korbin's mother looked up at me and back down at Kadence. "Okay, then. Why don't you go ahead and say goodbye to your father and meet me in the car." She smiled. "I'll be right behind you."

Kadence jumped into Korbin's arms. "Bye, Daddy." She wrapped her arms around his neck and hugged him tightly.

"Bye, munchkin. Be good for Nana."

He put her down, and she raised her hand in the air. "Good luck tonight. You've got this." She gave him a high-five.

He tousled her hair. "I'm gonna miss my little cheerleader."

She ran to me and hugged me around the waist. "Bye, Kailyn. I'll see you soon." She ran excitedly out the front door.

Korbin cleared his throat and extended a hand in my direction. "Mom, this is Kailyn." He pointed back at his mom. "Kailyn, this is my mother, Ella."

She stared at me through her black, thin-framed glasses then back up at him. She was much shorter than him, and her hair was marbled with black and silver.

I took a step closer and reached my hand out to her. "Nice to meet you, Mrs. Hart," I said nervously.

"Mom," Korbin, urged.

She reached out to shake my hand hesitantly. "Nice to meet you, Kailyn."

The awkward exchange made me uncomfortable, but I tried to look at myself through her eyes. I'm sure it hurt to see another woman with Korbin and Kadence.

"Nice to meet you, too." I smiled.

She looked at Korbin. "I hate to rush, but I don't want to leave Kadence waiting in the car." She grabbed her purse off of the entry-way table and stretched up to give Korbin a kiss on the cheek. "Bye, honey. Be careful tonight," she reminded.

"Always." Korbin kissed her on the cheek.

She opened the front door and stopped. "It was nice to meet you, Kailyn." She walked out the door and closed it behind her.

I sighed. "Well, that went well."

"She'll come around. It'll be okay." He gazed out the window, watching her drive away. "We just have to give her and the rest of my family time to adjust." He rubbed my arms. "We did kind of go from zero to sixty pretty quickly. They'll come around," he promised.

I hope so…

Dropping his hands by his sides, he walked toward the front door. "I'm leaving now. I have to meet Zach at the arena to get prepped for the ride." He grabbed his hat from the hook and placing it on his head. "I'll see you later." He walked out the door and left me even more confused.

Did he mean *see you later* as in at the rodeo or *see you later* as in when he gets back home? He still never *officially* asked me to go to the rodeo. Maybe he didn't want me there. Then again, I wasn't sure if I wanted to be there. The thought of him getting hurt made me shudder.

The longer I thought about the rodeo, the more I wanted to go. Even if it was hard to watch, the rodeo was a part of who Korbin is, and I needed to see him do the one thing he was most passionate about. Well, second to being a father.

Leesa offered to pick me up and go with me so I didn't have to go alone.

I went upstairs to get dressed and paired my favorite blue maxi dress with my new black cowgirl boots.

"Kailyn?" Leesa called from downstairs.

"I'm up here," I yelled. "I'll be down in a minute."

Grabbing my phone from the bathroom counter, I turned the bathroom light off and headed downstairs.

Leesa walked through the living room and scanned the house. "This places is beautiful," she cooed. "Wow, no wonder you wanted to live here."

I laughed. "It is very nice. Now, let's go before we're late."

She frowned. "Okay, but you have to show me more of this house later."

I locked the door and closed it behind me before making my way to Leesa's car.

I'd never been to a rodeo before, so I wasn't sure what to expect, and I was nervous for Korbin. Thinking about him on top of the angry beast had my stomach in knots. I was nervous but excited to see him in his element. The only other thing I worried about was how Korbin would feel about me being there.

Should I text him I'm coming or just show up and surprise him?

I wasn't sure how he would react to my being there, but I was going anyway.

We pulled up to the stadium. Large, bright lights lit up the dirt-filled pit through the darkened sky. We took a seat halfway up the bleachers, center of the arena, so we could see the action more clearly.

My heart pounded against my ribs as the announcer introduced one of the riders. An alarm sounded, and the gate flew open. The massive bull bucked the cowboy off after four seconds and flung him through the air like a rag doll. I gasped and covered my mouth with my hand. Surely they didn't actually enjoy this. They could get seriously hurt. Or killed.

The cowboy got up and ran toward the fence to escape the bull, hanging his head in frustration as he made his way back through the stalls and behind the gate.

Leesa cheered and pumped her fist in the air.

"How do you enjoy this?" I frowned at her.

"Honey, this is the country life." She shrugged one shoulder. "Rodeos are a big deal here, and they bring in a lot of money for our community." She frowned. "Korbin is our hometown superstar, and if you're going to get involved with him, you will have to get used to this." She scanned all the people in the crowd. "He's one of the top-ranked riders in the world, and this is his life. Almost everyone comes to these things just to watch him."

I nodded. She was right.

As the night continued, I watched as cowboy after cowboy came out and were thrown around the arena. Almost all of them ended the same—cowboy face down in the dirt, lucky to be alive.

When the announcer called Korbin's name, my heart

sank. The crowd around me roared with whistles, claps, and a lot of yelling women. I sat there, unable to move, horrified as he mounted the bull's back and wrapped the braided rope tightly around his hand. He scanned the crowd, stopping when his eyes landed on me. My breath caught. His blue eyes sparkled like gems under the brim of his cowboy hat.

A moment later, he broke our eye contact, threw his free hand up in the air, and nodded he was ready to go. I grabbed my stomach and waited for the gate to open. The clock started as soon as the two-thousand pound bull was through the gate.

Grabbing the edge of the bleachers, I clenched onto them until my hands burned, watching as it bucked over and over again. Eight seconds seemed like an eternity. After seven point six seconds, Korbin was tossed off. The crowd gasped in disbelief, and by the whispers behind me, it seemed as if Korbin hadn't been tossed off of a bull in two seasons of riding. That's what made him the best. He'd almost always made it until the buzzer.

He jumped up and grabbed his side with his hand, wincing in pain, but he looked okay enough. I was relieved and very worried. Maybe this life wasn't for me. I wasn't sure if I could stomach the fear of losing him to anything, especially an angry bull.

Korbin limped over to the gate, took his hat off, and threw it to the ground in a fit of anger. He was pissed. After the bull was secured, he stepped down off the gate, picked his hat up, and headed for the exit.

I nudged Leesa. "I'll be right back."

Stepping down the bleachers, I ran to catch up with him. "Korbin, wait!" I called as I approached him in the darkened area behind the stalls. "Are you okay?" I asked, scanning him for any obvious injuries.

He squinted his eyes and pinched the bridge of his nose. "Yes. I'm fine," he growled, dusting his jeans off.

I took a step back. "Wait...are you mad at me?" And if he was, why? I didn't do anything. "I just wanted to make sure you were okay."

He turned and I followed him behind the bleachers.

"No. Hell, I should've had that eight seconds. Dammit!" he yelled, pacing back and forth. Spinning on his heel, he stepped closer. "What do you want, Kailyn? Why're you here? I don't need any distractions right now."

Distractions? Was he blaming *me* for *him* falling off the bull? And was that all I was to him? A distraction from the hell he'd been living for the past year?

Narrowing my eyes at him, I propped my hand on my hip. "I came because I wanted to watch you do what you love!" I shouted back. "Are you saying it's *my* fault you didn't make it the full eight seconds?" I scoffed.

He shook his head and kicked the dirt beneath his boots. "I don't know what I'm saying. All I know is...I should *not* have failed. I've let down a lot of people in my life and I'm over feeling like a failure." He threw his hands out by his sides. "Bull riding is the *one* thing in my life that I've never failed at!" he roared. "Until now."

He scanned the arena as the next rider mounted his bull.

His breathing slowed and he tilted his head back, exhaling. Carefully, I stepped closer and placed my palm against his chest. "You are not a failure. You're the heart of country, Korbin. You encompass everything country stands for. You're strong, caring, fearless, and a damn good bull rider," I assured him. "I'm sorry. I should've asked you if I could come tonight."

His facial expression softened, his eyes kind. He sighed and caressed my cheek with his weathered hand. "I'm not fearless, Kailyn. I can ride a bull for eight seconds and be fearless, but my feelings for you scare the hell out of me." He stepped back and searched my eyes with his gentle gaze. "Sometimes I look at you and feel like I'm losing all control. Like my life is falling apart." He dropped his head.

As soon as the words left his mouth my stomach ached and my heart sank.

Caring about me makes him feel like his life is falling apart? I wasn't sure if that was an insult or a compliment.

He glanced back up as if he had something else to say, but then he turned to walk away. I wasn't going to let him walk away without dealing with this. He couldn't just walk away when things get tough.

Lurching toward him, I blurted, "Have you ever stopped to think, for just one second, that maybe your life isn't actually falling apart, Korbin? Maybe your life is falling into place just as it should be?" Tears stung my eyes.

He froze and I stood there, staring at the back of his head, willing him to turn around. My throat tightened with emotion, and my chest heaved with each quickened breath.

When he turned to face me, his gaze was harsh. As we stared at each other, he was trying to comprehend what I'd just said. His eyes narrowed.

He stepped closer and pointed a finger to his chest. "Are you saying my wife dying was meant to be?" he asked, his voice filled with anger and pain.

"That's not fair," I said bitterly, shaking my head.

He exhaled a shaky breath. "You have no idea how hard it is to be around you." He rubbed the back of his neck. "To feel the way I do when I look into your eyes, or when I'm with you." He paused and grabbed my arms, then continued, "I didn't want to feel this way, and I don't want to feel guilty about my feelings for you, but I don't know how not to." He took a step back, extended his arms out by his sides then slapped them on the sides of his dusty jeans. "Dammit! I don't know what else you want me to say, Kailyn. I really don't."

My lips tightened into a thin line as I contemplated my next words. I knew I had to be careful, because everything I said seemed to upset him. Then, I decided he was a grown man and I wasn't going to sugarcoat my feelings just to make him feel better. I knew he was hurting inside, and I hated that, but he had to know the truth and make a decision.

Stepping toward him, I brought my finger to my chest. "I want you to take a chance. To let your guard down. Let me in." He looked away, but I stepped around to grab his attention again. "I want you to say *I'm* worth it." I pointed to him and back to myself. "That *we're* worth giving this, whatever this is, a shot." My chin trembled and my throat tightened. "I want you to say you need me as much as I need you. I want you to say you love me as much as I love you." I gasped as soon as the words left my lips.

I knew I was falling for Korbin, but I hadn't realized until now that I was in love with him. *Oh, boy.*

As he peeked at me from under the brim of his hat, I waited and gauged his face for a reaction. "You're in love with me?" he breathed, leaning back on his heels.

We stood there, staring at each other. Both of us

breathing heavily. "Yes," I answered nervously. "I'm sorry. I know it's too soon..."

His jaw tightened and he took his hat off. Before I could even form another thought, he pushed me under the bleachers until my back was against the cold metal pole. Grabbing my face in his hands, he kissed me with an urgency that made my head spin. Butterflies whirled around in my stomach and my entire body tingled.

He wrapped one arm around my waist and pulled me tighter against him. My mouth yielded to his as he deepened the kiss. Looping two fingers through his belt loops, I pulled back just as much to meet his hips with mine. Feeling him against me. Feeling how much he wanted me.

Breaking the kiss, he pressed his forehead against mine. "Let's go," he whispered gruffly. Taking me by the hand, he pulled me toward his truck. "We'll come back for your car tomorrow," he said, assuming I'd driven there myself.

"I didn't drive" I shrugged. "Leesa drove me."

He jerked the door open and helped me in. "Even better."

I smiled as he eagerly closed the door and ran around to the other side.

He started up the truck and pulled out of the parking lot. "Where are we going?" I asked.

"Home," he said matter-of-factly as he pulled onto the dark and empty road ahead.

Pulling my phone out of my purse, I sent Leesa a quick text, telling her I had left with Korbin, so she wouldn't worry then I relaxed against the cool leather seat and stared out the window into the darkness.

Korbin was quiet on the way home and I was too afraid to talk about what had just happened. He didn't say he loved me, too, which was fine, but he really didn't say anything in response to my declaration. The anticipation of what was to come was tearing up my heart. I only hoped, when we arrived back home, things wouldn't be awkward.

Minutes later, we pulled up to the house and Korbin turned the engine off. Gripping the steering wheel, he laid his head back onto the headrest for a moment and stared out the windshield. "This is my reality now. This is my life." He glanced over at me. "I'm damaged inside, but I'm slowly starting to feel whole again."

I shifted my body toward him. "I'd like to explore this and see where it goes. I feel we're worth fighting for. We've both been through hell and deserve to be happy." I reached over to grab his hand. "So why not be happy together?"

He sucked in a deep breath and nodded. "Okay."

Korbin rounded the truck and opened my door. I jumped down onto the gravel drive. He walked behind the truck and grabbed a bag from the back, then he grinned and motioned for me to follow him. I ambled behind him in silence as we rounded the house and strolled alongside the bubbling creek only a few feet away from us. The full moon, and plethora of stars above, lit up our surroundings just enough to barely see each other.

He stopped at a large tree by the water and opened up his bag, pulling out an oversized plush blanket. He spread it out on the ground over some crumpled fall leaves. "I'm really sorry about earlier." He turned toward me. "You didn't deserve that."

I tried searching his eyes, but it was too dark. After spreading the blanket, he motioned for me to sit.

Kicking my boots off, I sat down on the soft fabric. "I get it. I've caused so much chaos and confusion in your life."

As the sounds of nature and water surrounded us, he slipped his boots off and sat down beside me.

"Maybe a little bit of chaos," he chuckled playfully. He picked something up off the ground and threw it into the creek, enveloped by the darkness. "You've opened my eyes to a lot of things." He grabbed my hand. "Not to mention, you jumped all in with Kadence, too, and she likes you so much already. I can tell."

I smiled at the thought of Kadence. The thought of possibly being a stepmother one day never really crossed my mind until now. Korbin and Kadence were a package deal and I was more than okay with that. I knew it wouldn't be easy, but I was willing to try.

Glancing over at me, he tilted his head slightly and grinned. "What're you doing to me?" He pondered the thought for a moment and continued to look at me.

Feeling powerful, I crawled over and straddled him. "I hope I'm showing you it's possible to love again," I said, wrapping my arms around his neck.

Leaning in, I kissed his neck just below his ear. He moaned and wrapped one arm around my waist, pulling me tighter against him. Reaching down, I grabbed the bottom of his shirt and pulled it over his head.

He leaned in, pushed my hair to the side, and kissed the dip between my neck and shoulder. His fingers slipped beneath my dress and he pulled it over my head and threw it on the blanket.

My mind was on him and only him, until a thought crossed my mind, wondering if he'd ever made love to his wife here. It wasn't healthy to keep comparing our relationship to theirs, but I couldn't help it sometimes. Pushing the thought from my head, I concentrated on Korbin and enjoyed the moment.

I shivered as the cool air blew across my skin. Goosebumps prickled my arms and legs as he reached behind me and unsnapped my bra with one swift movement. Grinding my center against his, I threw my head back and moaned as he bit my nape playfully.

He swiveled around, easing me onto my back. Reaching up, my fingertips tingled as I fumbled with his belt buckle. He quickly assisted me by jerking his belt off then he pulled my panties down my legs, kissing my thighs as he went. He looked up at me and I barely made out a grin.

Damn darkness. I can barely see him.

As he hovered over me, I quickly unbuttoned his pants and shimmied them, and his underwear, down just enough to free him. The anticipation had me reeling and I wasn't sure why I was so nervous. We'd already slept together, so it wasn't like I didn't know what to expect. Maybe it was the fact that I'd just told him I loved him. This time felt different. It was different. It was more intimate and we had a stronger connection. A part of me knew once we had sex again, my feelings would only get stronger. I just hoped he was okay with that and would catch up soon.

He positioned himself between my legs as one of his hands reached up to cup my wrist and hold it to the ground. A euphoric surge of ecstasy traveled through my entire body as he entered me, making me tremble. Even through the darkness, the passion and desire in his gaze was evident. He kissed my chin, up my jaw line, and down to my favorite spot below my ear. I rocked my hips to meet his with each thrust. He moaned into my ear, spreading more goosebumps across my skin. Through hooded eyes, I looked up at the clear sky, each star sparkling like silver glitter on a black canvas.

With each thrust, tension built deep in my belly and between my thighs. I grazed my nails down his back and tightened around him, making him moan once more. "No going back," he whispered into my ear.

We both found our release together, and I moaned, whispering, "No going back."

Chapter Thirteen

Kailyn

I AWAKENED THE NEXT morning in my own bed with a smile on my face. The last thing I remembered was falling asleep under the stars while listening to the water roll over the rocks. Korbin must have carried me to bed.

I rolled over, expecting to find Korbin, but the spot next to me was empty.

Getting out of bed, I pulled my silk robe over my shoulders and tied it in the front, then I padded down the hall to Korbin's bedroom. "Korbin," I called out, pushing the door open.

He was nowhere to be found, but I figured he was outside practicing for his next ride tonight. Looking up, I noticed the large photo of his wife that had been hanging above the bed was no longer there. He'd taken it down. There was also a box of letters and newspaper clippings on the bedside table.

I knew I shouldn't pry, but I walked over and pulled out

one of the newspaper articles and began reading. I only read the title and something struck me. *Local woman killed in head-on collision. Leaves grieving husband and daughter behind.* My hands trembled as I held the black and white piece of paper between my fingers. As I glanced at the date of the accident, a knot formed in my throat and the pit of my stomach. *September 10th.*

Blinking rapidly, I dropped the faded black and white paper, watching it float to the ground. *It couldn't be...*

Grabbing my stomach, I fell back onto the bed. "No," I whispered. "No."

Visions of that night clouded my mind. The headlights of the other car. The screeching of the tires sliding across the pavement. The sound of glass shattering all around me. The smell of burnt rubber and gasoline. I'd always known there was another car involved, but I was never told who it was or what had happened to the other people. I actually demanded no one tell me.

After a moment, I ran to the bathroom and hugged the toilet as my stomach lurched. I was going to be sick. "It can't be," I mumbled.

After gathering myself enough to stand, I stalked back over to the box and pulled out what looked like crime scene photos. Two pieces of mangled metal wrapped around one another with glass everywhere. One of the cars I recognized as being the car Mason had rented.

"Oh, God," I cried, hugging the piece of paper to my chest. The accident I was in a year ago had been the accident that killed Korbin's wife.

I can't believe this is happening. I had no idea...

I knew I'd have to tell Korbin, or, even worse, what if he

already knew and that's why he wasn't there when I woke up?

Dizziness consumed me as I tried to wrap my mind around everything. If Korbin didn't know, how was I supposed to tell him? How do you tell the man you've fallen in love with that you're the reason his wife is dead? Guilt washed over me. I may not have been driving that night, but I was still in the other car.

"Kailyn?" Korbin called from downstairs. "Are you awake?"

Jumping up, I quickly put the article and photos back in the box where I'd found them. I returned to the bathroom and splashed cold water on my face, trying to hide the fact that I'd just been sobbing moments earlier. I knew I had to tell him the truth about the accident, but I had to decide how and when to tell him. Hell, I wasn't even sure I'd fully processed it all myself.

"Kailyn?" he repeated as he walked into the bedroom.

"I'm in here," I called from the bathroom, trying to keep my voice strong.

Bending over the sink, I splashed more water on my face and hoped it was enough to hide my blood shot, puffy eyes.

He came up behind me, wrapping his strong arms around my waist. "There you are," he crooned.

He doesn't know. There's no way he knows.

Jumping slightly, I reached for a towel to dry my face.

"Are you okay?" he asked carefully, pulling away.

Looking up at him through the mirror, I smiled. "Yeah. I'm fine," I lied. "I came in here looking for you and thought I'd wash my face really quick." I shrugged. "I got some soap in my eyes." I blinked rapidly so the soap idea would seem believable.

His brows furrowed and I wasn't sure he believed me, but he didn't question it. "I have a lot to get done around the ranch before I head out for my next ride tonight. You're coming, right?" he asked with concern in his eyes.

I smiled, trying to keep my chin from trembling. "Of course. Wouldn't miss it."

"Great." He grinned like a little boy whose crush just checked yes on his *do you like me* note. "I'll meet you there, because I know you have a lot of work to do today. Don't forget you're bringing Kadence, too. She'll be home from my mom's around five-thirty." He turned to leave but stopped in the doorway. Our eyes met through the mirror again. "Last night was eye-opening for me. Thank you," he said, tenderly, then he left.

His words sliced right through me as I knew the truth I'd just discovered would gut him. I was sure he wouldn't forgive me once he found out and I couldn't say that I would blame him.

Walking over to close the bathroom door, I slowly slid down the sturdy wood until I was sitting on the floor. Hugging my knees to my chest, I cried, trying to rid myself from the guilt that was eating me alive. I wished I'd never picked up that newspaper article. I wished I could forget what I'd read and go back to feeling pure bliss with Korbin. Bliss that I'd quite possibly never feel with him again after tonight.

I couldn't forget, though. I'd never forget.

Wiping my eyes again, I gathered myself the best I could and went to get changed for work. Despite what I was feeling, I still had a lot of paperwork to do for the ranch and payroll to finish for the farm hands.

I was going to tell Korbin about the accident—just not

now. After the rodeo. I knew I had to tell him after his ride.

It was late afternoon and I hadn't accomplished much while combing through the files in my office. I stared at the computer screen, counting the number of times the cursor blinked on the Excel sheet. My mind wasn't where it needed to be. I couldn't focus on anything but that damn newspaper article.

Sighing in frustration, I stood from my desk and went out to the stalls to check on the horses.

As I turned the corner, Snowflake hung his head over the door and shook it to get my attention. I looked around for Korbin. When I didn't see him, I slowly walked over to him.

"Hey there, Snowflake," I said, stopping just shy of the door. I couldn't get over how big and shiny he was. Looking into his bulging eyes, I thought about Korbin's late wife. "I really messed up, Snowflake. What do I do now?" I asked him, as if I expected him to answer me. I wanted to reach out and pet him, but I knew Korbin's rule about it. "I'm sorry. I can't," I sighed. "Maybe one day..."

After checking on the rest of the animals, I returned to the office to work.

Crunching numbers had always been my strength, until now. My mind just wasn't in it. After an hour of getting nowhere, I decided to call it quits and get ready for Korbin's competition.

Around six-thirty, I met up with Leesa at the Rodeo again. I tried hiding my anxiety, but she saw right through me. "Kail. You're so quiet. What's wrong?" she asked, prodding me.

"Nothing. I'm fine," I replied, looking over at Kadence as she played with some of the other kids in an open field off in the distance.

She placed her hands on her hips. "Don't lie to me. I've been your best friend long enough to know when something is bothering you. Spill it."

I swallowed, looking around one last time to make sure nobody was within ear shot of us. "Okay. I found something out this morning. Something pretty devastating," I said.

She narrowed her eyes and nodded for me to continue.

Taking a deep breath, I continued, "I found out I'm the reason Korbin's wife is dead." My voice wavered against my will. "I'm the reason Kadence no longer has a mother," I blurted.

My hands trembled by my side as I talked.

She swallowed hard, but didn't seem as surprised as when I'd found out. "It's not your fault."

I dropped my head. "Yes it is. She died the same night we were driving back from your wedding reception," I said. "Leesa, Korbin was driving the other car that Mason hit," I blurted out. "Korbin's wife is dead because of me."

"What did you say?" The voice behind me was deep.

My heart sank as I turned to find Korbin standing only a few feet behind me. His eyes were wide, his skin pale, all the color drained from his face.

Oh, God..."Korbin! I'm. Wait. Let me explain."

I reached out to grab his hand, but he pulled away and stepped back. The look in his eyes made me sick to my stomach. He was disgusted. What had I done?

"You were driving the other car that night?" he whispered hoarsely.

"No." I shook my head fiercely. "I was in the car, but I wasn't driving."

He lifted a hand. "Stop, Kailyn. Just stop," he said, raising his voice.

He turned around, yanked his cowboy hat off, and ran a hand through his hair then over his face.

I stood there in shock. Not sure what to do or say. I wanted to explain, but I didn't know how.

He turned to face me once again, his face flush and eyes angry. "Have you known this entire time? Is that why you came here?" He stepped closer, rushing me. "Have you been feeling so guilty that you thought you'd come here and seduce me to make yourself feel better?" he spat at me. "Were you ever going to even tell me about this? Or were you just hoping I'd never find out and we could continue...this... whatever this is—or *was...*"

His words cut deeply, but I had to fix this. "No!" I yelled. "That's not what happened at all. My feelings for you are real, Korbin." I stretched my arms out by my side. "I just found out this morning. I swear. I was going to tell you after the rodeo. I didn't want you distracted during your ride."

"Distracted? A little late for that, don'tcha think?" he scoffed. "Wait. This morning?" he asked, shaking his head like he'd figured something out. "That's why you looked so upset this morning."

"Yes," I whispered, looking down at the gravel beneath my feet.

"Daaaddy!" Kadence called out as she ran over to hug Korbin.

Turning away, I quickly wiped my eyes before facing Kadence.

He picked her up and hugged her. "Hey, kiddo."

When his eyes cut back to me, my stomach roiled and nausea took over. The fury in his eyes was indescribable. I'd done that to him. *Me.* I wanted more than anything to take it back. To have never gotten in the car that night. To have taken away Mason's keys and forbade him to drive.

"Good luck out there, Daddy." She gave him a kiss, then he put her back down on the ground.

He gave her a high-five and forced a smile. "Thanks, sweetie."

Kadence turned and grabbed my hand. "Kailyn, let's go find good seats so we can watch him."

"You know, Kadence," Korbin interrupted. "I want you to sit with Cowboy Zach tonight, okay?" He glanced up at me with an, *I dare you to challenge me* stare.

"But why?" She frowned. "I wanna sit with Kailyn."

Korbin cut his eyes to me, again, signaling for me to say something. "It's okay." I forced a smile through the tears welling under my lashes. "I'll sit behind you and Cowboy Zach, alright?" I promised.

"Okay, I guess." She kicked the gravel beneath her feet. "I'm gonna go get Cowboy Zach and pick a spot up front. I'll see you in there."

Korbin turned and started to walk away, but he stopped, his voice harsh as he said, "I want you gone. Out of our lives.

Take your stuff and just go."

I gulped my own hurt down and hoped he was only reacting.

He needed to cool down. I couldn't let him get on that bull. "Korbin, wait," I called out to him. "You can't go out there and ride like this. Your mind isn't in the right place. It doesn't make sense to go out there right now."

He stopped and turned to face me. "Right now, Kailyn, getting on that bull is the only damn thing that does makes sense."

My vision blurred beneath the tears I could no longer stop. "Please, Korbin. I'm so sorry…" I said, feeling defeated as each warm tear rolled softly down my cheeks.

He looked at me with eyes full of sadness and disappointment. "So am I."

My shoulders shook as I cried, watching him disappear behind the gates.

"Kail, I'm so sorry." Leesa hugged me. "Do you want me to take you home? You can stay with us again until we figure something out."

"Kailyn!" Kadence yelled from the bleachers. "Hurry up, It's about to start!"

I turned to Leesa, took a deep breath, and wiped the tears from my eyes. "No. I need to stay here…for Kadence."

And for him. To make sure he was okay.

Leesa sighed. "But why are you torturing yourself like this?"

"Because. None of this is Kadence's fault. She deserves a proper goodbye from me." Kadence jumped up and down, clapping her hands. "I can't leave without telling her goodbye."

"Okay. Let's go." She may not have agreed with my

decision, but she stayed and supported me anyway.

KORBIN

I stood there, looking at the beast of a bull before me. He snorted and violently rammed the chute. He was the toughest bull to ride and had hurt many rodeo riders in the past. Bull riding was my comfort. It was my outlet. Eight seconds I didn't have to think or feel. An eight second escape from reality. A break from my own thoughts.

My mind was clouded with what had just happened with Kailyn. How could she not have told me the second she'd found out? Her boyfriend's drunk driving had resulted in me losing the love of my life and Kadence losing her mother. How was I supposed to feel about that? How was I supposed to look her in the eyes every day, knowing what I knew? I had no choice but to end things with her. I did the right thing.

With a deep breath, I climbed the steps in front of me and readied myself to mount the most feared bull in the Rodeo circuit. Cheers roared from the bleachers circling the ring. I scanned the crowd until my eyes locked with Kailyn's. She looked sad, scared, worried–all the things I was supposed to be feeling. But anger and adrenaline were all that coursed through my veins.

I broke eye contact with Kailyn and looked at Kadence. She clapped and rooted me on, smiling from ear to ear. I tipped my hat at her and forced a smile. Her eyes lit up with pride. She held three fingers up to sign *I love you*, then kissed her fingers and blew a kiss to me. That was something we'd done since she was a toddler. It was *our thing*. Something special just between us. I smiled and threw an *I love you* kiss back at her. Then I nodded at the handlers, signaling I was ready.

I mounted the bull and wrapped the rope around my hand, jerking on it to ensure I had a solid grip. The bull was already bucking behind the gate—he was ready to go. My pulse hammered in my ears. I took a deep breath and prepared for the ride of my life.

Holding my other hand up in the air, I nodded a second time. "Now!"

The gate swung open and that was it. No turning back. The angry bull bucked wildly as we entered the ring.

My hand burned against the rope as I squeezed, tightening my grip when I started to lose my balance. I'd only been on for a few seconds, but it felt like a lifetime. *Eight seconds*—I kept reminding myself. Just eight seconds.

The buzzer sounded at eight seconds, and just as I started to bail, the bull shifted and bucked so hard it threw me off, plummeting me to the dirt below.

Kailyn

Everyone cheered after the buzzer sounded, but the cheers turned to screams as we all watched him fly through the air like a rag doll. *Korbin, no!*

As soon as he hit the ground, the entire stadium went silent. Everyone watched in horror, waiting for him to get up. But he didn't move.

Two men gathered the bull and got him out of the ring as quickly as possible.

"Daddy! Why isn't he getting up?" Kadence shouted.

Without thinking, I reached over to hug her and covered her eyes with my arm. "It's okay. He's gonna be fine," I said, trembling and unable to blink as I continued watching the medical team.

Korbin laid lifeless on the ground for what seemed like hours, but I knew it had only been seconds or maybe minutes. Everyone watched, expecting him to jump up at any moment. But he didn't. He wasn't moving at all. My lungs burned, and I struggled to breathe as my chest tightened.

C'mon, Korbin. Get up. Please get up.

A few seconds later, an ambulance drove into the ring and two men got out and ran to Korbin's side. I turned to Leesa and saw the look of terror on her face. "Leesa. I need you to do me a huge favor," I pleaded with her.

"Anything," she whispered, eyes wide.

I tried to gather myself. "Take Kadence and meet us at the hospital. I'm going to ride there with the ambulance."

"No! I wanna go with Daddy!" Kadence cried. "Please!"

Emotion caught in my throat as I looked into her glossy eyes. "I know you do, honey, but they need to work quickly to help your daddy." I wiped a tear from her cheek and gave her a comforting hug.

"We'll be fine," Leesa promised. "We'll meet you at the hospital. Now go!"

I nodded, then leapt over rows of bleachers and ran into the ring full force. "Korbin!" I yelled.

"Whoa, miss," one of the guards said as he grabbed me around the waist and held me back.

"Please!" I pleaded. "I have to get to him!" My entire body collapsed into the man's arms and he slowly lowered me to the ground. I sat there on my knees and watched the paramedics work on Korbin.

Flashes of his face after he'd overheard the truth about the accident flooded my mind. He'd been so angry and distracted. I was the reason this had happened. That was exactly why I hadn't wanted him to find out until after the ride.

I also remembered him grinning at Kadence and tipping his hat before the gate opened. He loved her more than anything in the world. He had to pull through—for her.

Looking over to my right, I saw Korbin's cowboy hat lying on the ground. I forced myself to stand and walked over to pick it up. It was covered in dirt, but I didn't care. I hugged it to my chest and cried.

They quickly placed him on a backboard and loaded him into the ambulance.

"Miss, if you're going with us we have to go now," the paramedic interrupted.

"Yes, please, thank you," I blurted. I ran to the ambulance and sat on the bench beside Korbin, trying to stay out of the way so they could do their job to keep him alive.

They started an IV, pushed meds, and hooked him up to a monitor to keep track of his vital signs.

"Please, Korbin, wake up," I pleaded. I reached out to grab his limp hand with mine. "Please."

I'd never been so scared and uncertain about something in my life. I'd only known Korbin for a short time, yet I'd felt like I'd known him for years. We'd gotten close so fast, and I wasn't ready to lose him—even if I had already lost him emotionally. I had to at least make sure he was going to be okay. Then, if he still wanted me gone, I'd leave and be out of his life for good.

The ambulance ride was bumpy as we made our way to the hospital. It was only a few miles away, but it seemed like we were in the back of that ambulance for a lot longer than ten minutes.

When we arrived at the hospital, I exited quickly so they could get Korbin out as fast as possible. They ushered him quickly through the sliding glass doors. I ran after him, but a set of strong hands stopped me.

"Ma'am, I'm sorry. You'll have to wait in the waiting room. The doctor will come get you once they have an update."

They disappeared behind a heavy wooden door at the end of the hallway. A moment later, I heard Kadence behind me.

"Kailyn!" She ran up and threw her arms around my waist. "How's Daddy? Is he gonna be okay?"

I looked down into her big doe eyes, filled with tears, and made the decision that I couldn't lie to her. I bent down and rubbed both of her arms with my hands. "I don't know, honey. Your daddy was hurt pretty badly, but he has the best doctors and nurses helping him right now." I flashed a reassuring smile, trying to calm her. "They're taking good care of him, okay?"

I wasn't sure if I'd done the right thing, but I didn't want to lie to her. Everything was uncertain at that point and she deserved to know. I didn't want to create false hope.

She hugged me and buried her face into my shoulder as she cried. I looked up at Leesa who still looked like she was in shock. She frowned and got out her phone to call Jake to tell him what had happened.

"Come on," I said to Kadence. "Let's go sit down." We

walked over and took a seat in the oversized, green hospital chairs and waited. And waited. And waited. Every time the door opened, I jumped, anticipating news. And every time I was disappointed.

The clock on the wall read nine-thirty. My eyes focused on the second hand as it slowly made its way around, passing each number. Kadence fell asleep on my shoulder, clutching Korbin's dusty hat in her arms. Leesa had gone up to the desk multiple times, begging for an update, but they kept telling her they didn't have one. My stomach churned as a million scenarios raced through my mind.

About an hour later, Korbin's parents came rushing through the hospital door and up to the counter. "My son, Korbin Hart, he had an accident. Is he okay?" his mom said, without taking a breath. "What happened? What's going on?" she demanded. "Where's my son?"

Not wanting to wake Kadence, I lightly shifted her head over onto Leesa's shoulder and stood to meet his parents.

"Ella?" I whispered from behind her. "He's still in the back with the doctors."

Ella turned to me, her eyes wide with panic. "Is he okay?"

I sighed. "I'm not sure. The doctor hasn't come back out yet, and I doubt they'd tell me anything, anyway." I frowned.

Korbin's dad spoke up, "We got here as quickly as we could after getting the call."

Ella's eyes frantically searched the waiting room. "Oh my God. Kadence."

"She's fine." I pointed to the corner of the room. "I've got her. She's over there with Leesa, sleeping."

Her shoulders relaxed and she placed a hand over her heart. "Thank you."

The heavy wooden door opened, again, and this time a dark-haired doctor walked down the hallway toward us. "Hart family."

My heart sank. This was it.

"We're his parents." Ella pointed to herself and then to William. "I'm Ella and this is William."

I'd heard Korbin talk a lot about his dad and he looked just like him. Only a younger version with no gray hair.

"Is Korbin okay?" Ella asked quietly, almost unable to speak. She feared the worst. We all did.

He motioned for them to go into a room marked *Family Room*. "Let's go in here."

Just as they started to enter, Ella turned and nodded to me, giving me the okay to sit in with them. I exhaled a sigh of relief.

We entered the room hastily, anxious to hear an update. "Is he okay?" William asked.

I couldn't wait any longer. The silence was killing me. "Is he alive?" I shrieked.

Ella and William both glanced at me with tears in their eyes.

The doctor hugged a metal clipboard to his chest. "Korbin took a really hard hit to his head. He has internal bleeding and is in surgery to try to stop it. He's alive, but in critical condition." His brows furrowed and his lips formed a tight line. "I'm not sure what's going to happen, but you need to be prepared for anything."

I fell backward onto the chair behind me. My legs were numb and I couldn't fully focus on what he was saying. *How does anyone prepare for something like that?*

I sighed. "He's alive, though," I echoed. "He's gonna be

okay. He has to be," I said, trying to convince myself.

"When can we see him?" Ella asked.

The doctor placed a hand on Ella's arm. "One step at a time. We'll see how he does through the surgery and then he'll have to spend some time in recovery. After that, they'll move him into a room where you can visit with him briefly."

I stared at the wall, unable to respond to anyone or anything. My legs bounced nervously as I replayed the night in my mind and hoped Korbin would be okay.

The doctor walked toward the door and turned to face us again. "We're doing everything we can to make sure Korbin returns back home where he belongs. I promise to personally come get you the second he's out of surgery and in recovery, okay?"

"Thank you, doctor," Ella choked out.

He opened the door to leave. "I'll have one of the nurses put you into Korbin's room so you can get some rest while you wait. Once he's out of recovery, we'll wheel him back to his room so you can see him." He paused in the doorway. "I'll be back with an update shortly."

After the doctor left the room, Ella and William walked outside to get some fresh air and call family and friends to update them on what had happened.

I found Leesa in the waiting room and she searched my face for answers. Sitting down beside her, I whispered so I wouldn't wake Kadence. "He's alive." I sighed. "He's in surgery right now and in critical condition. They don't know what the outcome is going to be because he has internal bleeding and hit his head really hard," I said, trying to remember what all the doctor had just said.

"I'm so sorry, Kail." She grabbed my hand. "Is there

anything else I can do?"

I squeezed her hand. "Actually, you've done so much already. Thank you for everything." Although I was still worried about Korbin I was somewhat comforted in knowing he was alive. "You can go home now. I'll be okay. They're putting us in his room so we can rest while we wait."

"Are you sure?" She raised an eyebrow. "I don't mind staying."

"I know." I exhaled slowly. "I appreciate everything and I love you, but we'll be fine."

"Okay then. Call me as soon as you have an update. I don't care what time it is," she demanded.

"I will." I nodded absently. "I promise."

It was time to tell Kadence the news. "Kadence, wake up sweetie." I brushed her hair out of her face.

She groaned and yawned as she blinked herself awake. "Kailyn? What's wrong? Is Daddy okay?" Her sleepy eyes were full of worry.

Forcing a smile, I tried to calm her. "Your daddy is in surgery right now, and they're moving us to his room so we can see him when he's done, okay?"

"Okay," she said groggily.

I gave Leesa a hug then walked outside to get Ella and William. The hospital entryway was lit up with lights so bright, they reached the darkened parking lot.

"Nana!" Kadence piped up, running to Ella.

Well, she's awake now.

"Oh, Kadence, honey." Ella scooped her into her arms and kissed the top of her head.

I motioned inside. "They're ready to take us to his room."

I wasn't sure why, but I kept waiting for them to ask me

to leave.

Ella grabbed my arm to stop me. "I'm sorry I was stand-offish to you when I first met you." She frowned. "It's just hard seeing him with another woman."

The news about the accident would probably make her upset again, and I knew it wasn't my place to tell her. That would be up to Korbin to decide if he wanted anyone else to know.

Glancing down at the ground, I tried hiding my nerves. "It's okay. I understand."

She smiled as a tear rolled down her wrinkled cheeks. "He said you make him happy," she sniffled. "He said things were getting serious pretty quickly." She dabbed her cheeks with a tissue. "All I want is for my son and Kadence to be happy. He's been so distant and living in so much pain." She grabbed my hand. "As much as it hurts to see him with another woman. It also warms my heart to see him smiling again."

She hugged me then turned to Kadence. "Let's go inside and wait for your Daddy."

We all walked inside and waited for someone to take us to his room.

A nurse took us to a large room full of monitors and machines. On one side of the room there was a large window. Below that was a long bench with a pull-out bed. I grabbed the linens out of a small closet and got the bed ready for Kadence while Ella and William went to get some coffee.

"Will you lay with me and rub my head?" Kadence asked. "Mommy always used to lay with me and rub my head."

Guilt and worry rushed over me as I looked into her glassy chestnut eyes. She'd already lost her mother—she couldn't lose her father, too.

I slipped under the blankets beside her. "Sure."

She snuggled into me, and I wrapped one arm around her, pulling her close. With my other hand, I stroked her hair and stared at the door, waiting for someone to come in.

"Kailyn?" She blinked up at me.

"Yeah?" I replied, looking down at her.

"I'm scared. Are you scared?"

"Yes," I answered honestly. "It's okay to be scared."

She yawned. "I'm really glad you're here." She blinked heavily, finally drifting off to sleep.

"Me, too," I whispered. "Me, too."

Chapter Fourteen

Kailyn

THERE WAS A KNOCK on the door, jolting me awake. It was the doctor we'd seen in the waiting room. I wondered for a moment how long I'd been asleep.

Ella and William jumped to their feet and waited for him to speak.

"Good news," he said. "Korbin's out of surgery and has been in recovery for almost an hour already." He sighed. "Sorry it took me so long to get over here. I had an emergency in another room. You should be able to see him really soon."

We all sighed in unison. "Thank you, doctor," Ella said with a hopeful smile.

"Now, he's not out of the woods just yet," he warned us. "He's in a coma right now. We've stopped the bleeding and done everything we can do. Now it's up to him."

"We understand," William said, but I took his hopeful

smile as a good sign.

"They'll be bringing him in here shortly."

After he left, I relaxed back into the bed and woke Kadence.

"Hey," I whispered, gently shaking her awake.

She jumped up and looked around the room. "What's wrong? Where's Daddy?"

"He's out of surgery, and they're gonna bring him in to see us soon."

She perked up a little and got up to go to the bathroom.

Shortly after the doctor left, a nurse stood in the doorway and looked over at Ella and William. "There are some people downstairs in the waiting room asking about Mr. Hart. Would you like to go down and talk to them?" she asked with a comforting smile.

Ella wiped her nose with a tissue. "Yes. We'll quickly go update everyone."

William spoke up softly, "Kailyn, do you need anything? Coffee? Something to eat?"

I smiled and rubbed my arms. "I'm okay. Thank you, though."

"We'll be right back," Ella said. "I wrote my number down in case you need it before we get back." She handed me a small piece of paper.

Kadence came out of the bathroom and walked over to Ella as she was leaving. She rubbed her belly and frowned. "Nana, I'm really hungry."

William rubbed the top of her head. "Come on down with us, and we'll find you something to eat."

They turned to walk away, and I paced the floor waiting for Korbin.

Twenty minutes had passed. I glanced out the door, growing more anxious. Nurses and doctors hustled by, alarms sounded in the distance, call lights lit up the long hallway, and a patient was being transported by hospital bed, but it wasn't Korbin.

Finally, I saw another stretcher being pushed down the hallway. "Korbin," I whispered, tears filling my eyes. As soon as they entered the room, they started hooking him up to all of the machines. It took everything in me not to run to him, but I knew they had to get everything transferred from the portable monitors first.

Seeing him all beat up was hard. He had a large gash that had been sutured on his forehead, and the left side of his face was badly bruised. The sheet was pulled up to his chin, so I couldn't assess the rest of him. I quickly picked my phone up and sent a text to Ella.

The nurses disconnected more wires from a portable monitor on his bed and plugged them into the stationary monitor on the wall behind the bed. "If you need anything at all just push the call button." She pointed toward the bed and smiled.

They both left the room and shut the door behind them.

Taking Korbin's hand in mine, I sat in the chair beside his bed. The beeping of the machines, and the sound of oxygen flowing through his breathing tube filled the room. I counted each time the electrocardiogram displayed his heartbeat.

"Korbin, if you can hear me…it's Kailyn. I'm here." I squeezed his hand gently. "Kadence and your parents are here, too. We're all worried about you and ready for you to wake up."

I failed to hold back tears no matter how hard I tried.

Flashes of him flying through the air and hitting the ground invaded my mind, and I trembled as I relived that moment.

Standing up, I pushed the thought from my mind, bent over, and kissed him lightly on the forehead. "Korbin Hart, you listen to me," I whispered. "You may be mad at me right now, and that's okay, but you have to fight. You have a daughter who needs you. Do you hear me?" Tears escaped my eyes and landed on the pillow by his head. "Don't you dare give up on her. She can't lose you, too."

The door flung open, and Kadence ran inside, followed by Ella and William. "Daddy!" Kadence yelled.

Quickly wiping the tears from my eyes, I moved to the side, so they could get closer to him. "Can I touch him?" Kadence asked wearily.

"Yeah, sweetie," I pointed at the wires connected to various parts of his body. "Just be careful not to touch any of those or the tube coming out of his mouth. You can grab his hand. I bet he'd like that."

She hesitated. "Why's he hooked up to all this stuff?" Her chin trembled. "I don't like it."

William bent down and rubbed her arms. "I know it's scary, but he needs these things, so the nurses and doctors can keep him safe and monitor him."

She turned back to Korbin and slowly rubbed the top of his hand. "Can he hear me?" she asked, looking up at me.

"Sure," I said, my heart breaking as I watched her. "I'd like to think so."

She turned back to look at him. "Daddy. I love you. Please don't die," she cried, leaning over to kiss the top of his hand. "I love you so much, Daddy. You can't die. Please don't leave me like mommy did," she pleaded through sobs.

My heart shattered into a million pieces. I wished I could take her pain away. Even though she wasn't my daughter, I hated seeing her so upset.

Looking behind me, I saw William had his arms wrapped around Ella as she cried against his chest. It was hard on them to see Kadence so upset, too.

Turning my attention back to Kadence, I turned her around and placed my hands on her shoulders. "Kadence, your daddy loves you more than anything in this world. He's going to fight with everything he has to stay here with you. Do you hear me?" I asked, quickly wiping a tear from her cheek.

She nodded and wrapped her arms around me.

Korbin Hart *is*, afterall, the heart of country. He was a fighter. A strong, stubborn, and determined cowboy. I had to believe he was going to be okay—that we were all going to be okay—no matter what.

Chapter Fifteen

Kailyn

One Week Later

BLINKING THE SLEEP FROM my eyes, I tried to focus as the sun shone through the window, scorching my pupils. *Ugggh.* I groaned and arched my aching back. Sleeping on an uncomfortable hospital chair for a week was catching up to me, and my body hated me for it.

I glanced over at Korbin lying in the same position he'd been in for a week. Last night, the doctors had decided they were going to try taking him off the ventilator to see if he was able to breathe on his own. They'd already performed multiple spontaneous breathing trials with a little more success each time. It was a big moment for everyone because it would tell a lot about his condition and what the outcome would be.

Standing up, I stretched, looking out of the large window at the snow-capped mountains in the distance. I couldn't help but think back to the argument I'd had with Korbin before his ride. I'd never forget the look of disgust and hurt in his eyes. I hadn't realized just how badly I'd wanted him and how much I loved him until that moment, when I saw I'd completely lost him and any chance we'd had for a future together.

A light touch on my shoulder startled me. "Kailyn," Ella said.

I turned to face her. "Good morning," I said, rubbing my eyes. "I'm sorry, I didn't hear you come in."

She frowned. "You look tired. Have you even left the hospital at all?"

I began to yawn and covered my mouth. "No. I've been showering here, and Leesa has brought my clothes and necessities by." Walking over to the bed, I grabbed Korbin's hand. "It's okay, though. I really don't want to leave until I know he's okay."

William walked in with Zach and Max, Korbin's best friends.

He handed me a cup of coffee and smiled. "I thought you could use this."

Wrapping my hands around the cup, I brought it to my nose and inhaled the robust coffee. My only saving grace while staying in the hospital with Korbin. The steam drifted up, touching my cheeks.

I was so grateful. "Thank you."

As I started to take a sip, the doctor came in with two nurses behind him. "It's time." He frowned and glanced over at the monitors behind the bed. "The good news is, he's made some progress over the past few days." He opened Korbin's file. "His last Coma Scale score was a three, and now he's up to a nine." He smiled. "He's making great progress, and if he continues, he can come out of this with a full recovery."

We all sighed before walking over to Korbin's bed.

"That's great news," Max said, placing his hand on Korbin's knee. "We're all here, man."

We surrounded his bed and looked at each other. None of us knew what was going to happen, but we were all in it together and all hoped for the best. Kadence wasn't present because we weren't sure what the outcome would be.

My palms were sweaty, and my body ached with anticipation as the doctor and nurses took their places by the monitors.

"Okay." Ella wiped a tear from her cheek. "We're ready."

The doctor and nurses talked quietly back and forth with each other as the doctor started weaning him off the breathing machine. One nurse watched the monitor and made notes on a clipboard. My mind was foggy, and I was in a daze, terrified Kadence could possibly lose her father.

The monitor on the wall started blaring, breaking me from my thoughts.

"Wha-what's going on?" Ella cried.

The doctor instructed the other nurse to wait as she started to push meds through Korbin's IV. Everyone froze, and it was as if the air had been sucked out of the room. I couldn't understand why everyone was just standing there watching the monitor as his oxygen saturation dropped.

The doctor listened to Korbin's lungs through his stethoscope. "Come on."

Maybe it was selfish of me, but I hadn't spent over a week in the hospital with him only to watch him die. He was going to walk out of this hospital and hold Kadence in his arms again.

Leaning down, I begged him. "Korbin. Wake up. Please wake up." I cried. "Fight, dammit."

Tears rolled down my cheeks and landed on his.

"SATS are coming up, doctor," one of the nurses said. "Seventy-nine percent and climbing."

A moment later, she placed a stethoscope against his side. "Oxygen is up to ninety percent and twelve respirations."

The other nurse watched the monitor. "Heartrate is ninety."

William clapped his hands together. "That a boy, Korbin!" He grabbed a handkerchief from his shirt pocket and dabbed his eyes. "He's a fighter, alright."

I fell back onto the chair by the bed. "So...he's gonna be okay?"

The doctor nodded. "He's breathing on his own now." He shined a light in each of Korbin's eyes. "We'll have to do more tests. He's not out of the woods, just yet, but it's looking promising." He wrote something in Korbin's file then took a moment to listen to his breathing again.

Max pulled his phone out. "I'm gonna step outside and update the band on what's been going on. They've been worried about him."

Zach pulled his phone out and swiped his finger across the screen. "I need to step out, too. My phone has been blowing up with texts from our rodeo buddies and the other farm hands wanting an update." A look of relief crossed his face. "I'll be back shortly."

Ella and William walked toward the door. "We need to go call the rest of our family and friends to update them on his progress." She smiled. "We'll be back."

Nodding to them, I smiled as they left the room. Then,

I sent out a quick text to Leesa, letting her know what had happened.

One of the nurses came over and placed a hand on my back. "Honey, why don't you go home and get some rest. You haven't left the hospital since the day you arrived."

"Thank you, but I can't." I glanced at Korbin. "Not until he's awake, and I know he's okay."

She smiled softly. "Well, I wanted to at least try. Let me know if I can get you anything." She turned back around. "He's lucky to have you."

After that, the rest of the staff left the room, and I sat by the bed like I had for the past week and prayed for a miracle.

Chapter Sixteen

A NOTHER WEEK HAD GONE by, and the amount of visitors had begun to dwindle. Less phone calls came through, less cards, flowers, and balloons arrived, but I made sure Korbin was never alone.

Cowboy Zach, as Kadence called him, made sure the ranch was physically taken care of while I was at the hospital. I knew the ranch was Korbin's life, his pride and joy, so I took care of the rest from my laptop until he could get back home.

Home. That's exactly where he needed to be.

In the past two weeks, I had read every card and letter that was sent to him, talked about the weather, and read the latest Rodeo leaderboard stats to him. Kadence popped in and out with Ella and William as much as possible and had decorated his room in colorful drawings she'd made for him.

Sitting down next to his bed, I grabbed his hand and looked up at the monitors to see everything was still normal. After a bit, my eyelids grew heavy. My mind was tired from lack of sleep. The room was dark except for his monitors and the illumination of the TV absently playing in the background. Looking at the clock on the wall, I groaned when I realized it was only nine o'clock. It felt like midnight.

Laying my head down on the side of the bed, I held his hand in mine and fell asleep.

I was having the best dream ever—or so I thought. There was pressure on my hand. "Korbin…" I blinked the sleep from my eyes and glanced down at my hand, realizing I wasn't dreaming. He squeezed my fingers again

Reaching over with my free hand, I jerked the emergency cord on the wall. "Somebody come in here, please!" I yelled toward the door. "Hurry! Please hurry!"

Two nurses rushed into the room. "What's wrong?" They simultaneously looked up at the monitor then back down at Korbin.

I wiped tears from my eyes. "He squeezed my hand." Adrenaline coursed through my body.

One of the nurses turned to the other. "Page Dr. Houston, STAT."

Bending over, I kissed Korbin's forehead. "Come on, Korbin. Open your eyes," I begged.

Minutes later, Dr. Houston ran into the room and rushed to the other side of the bed. He shined his tiny flashlight into Korbin's eyes and turned to the nurse behind him. "His pupils are reacting. Let's get him up to CT *now*."

I quickly moved to the corner of the room, so I wasn't in

the way. They wheeled him off, and I grabbed my phone off the counter. My heart pounded and my hands trembled as I called Ella to tell her the news.

Ella and William arrived with Kadence shortly after I called them. We all patiently waited for the CT results.

About thirty minutes later, Dr. Houston walked into the room. "Good news." He nodded to William and Ella. "Korbin's CT shows no more bleeding, and the swelling is down. Now we just wait a little bit longer."

Sighing with relief, I fell back onto the chair by the window. *He's gonna be okay.* After all the days that had passed, I almost couldn't believe it.

Kadence bounced up and down, clapping her hands. "Daddy's gonna be okay?"

"It looks that way," the doctor said, patting her on the head. He glanced over at Ella. "If anything else changes just let us know. I'll be back around to check on him later."

William rushed over to shake Dr. Houston's hand. "Thank you so much, Doctor."

He smiled. "You don't have to thank me." He nodded at Korbin. "He's the one doing all the work."

Crossing my arms, I watched his chest rise and fall evenly with each breath. "He's a fighter," I whispered to myself.

The reception in the hospital was almost non-existent, so William and Ella had gone downstairs to make their rounds of updates. I was pretty sure the entire town was worried about Korbin due to the amount of phone calls they had to make each time there was a change.

Kadence laid back on one of the reclining chairs and fell asleep. I draped a sheet over her and sat by Korbin's bed as I waited for his parents to return.

"Kadie…" A hoarse whisper caught my attention.

At first, I couldn't move or react. I thought I had imagined it because I'd been so anxious for Korbin to wake up. A few seconds later, I realized I wasn't imagining it. Korbin blinked heavily as he stared up at the ceiling.

"Korbin!" I jumped up and grabbed his hand. "It's Kail. Kadence is here, too."

I jerked the emergency cord again and yelled toward the nurse's station across the hall. "He's awake!"

My yelling scared Kadence awake, and she ran over to the bed. "Daddy! Daddy are you okay?"

Picking Kadence up, I leaned over so he could see us. We both cried as he blinked up at us—his eyes struggling to adjust. He was too weak to turn his head, but that was okay. We were just relieved he was awake.

Smiling down at him, I sucked in a deep breath and sighed. I could finally breathe again. The weight of the unknown was no longer on my mind, and all of the emotions I'd tried to hold back for the past couple of weeks finally boiled over. I couldn't hold them in any longer.

"You're gonna be okay, Korbin." I gently ran my fingers through his hair. "You're gonna be okay."

Kadence sniffled. "Yeah, Daddy. You're gonna be okay. Easy peasy."

KORBIN

Blinking up at the bright lights above me, I tried to focus.

Where am I?

Turning my head, I noticed a nurse hanging a new bag of saline on my IV pole. The last thing I remembered was being thrown off the bull.

"Good morning, Mr. Hart," the nurse said. "How're you feeling?"

Groaning, I touched my pounding head.

"Easy now." She grabbed my hand and pushed it back down by my side. "You're gonna be okay, but you can't over do it right now."

"What happened?" My mind was still a little foggy.

"You've been in a coma for the past two weeks." She patted my shoulder. "Dr. Houston was in here earlier and told you about it. It's okay, though, it will take some time for your memories to come back." She frowned. "Your body has been through a lot."

That's right. I remembered the doctor being in the room now.

"And, Kadence?" *Where's my girl? I need to see her.*

"Your daughter's just fine." She smiled warmly. "Your parents have been bringing her by every day to see you." She reached over to fluff my pillow and raised the head of the bed slightly. "Kailyn hasn't left the hospital since your accident. We kept telling her to go home to get some rest, but she wouldn't until she knew you were going to be okay. You're lucky to have her." She walked to the other side of the room, took her gloves off, and threw them in the trashcan by the door. "I'll be back soon to check on you again. Just push that red button there by your side if you need anything."

Lost in my own thoughts, I contemplated what the nurse said about Kailyn. My memories may have been foggy, but I hadn't forgotten about our argument before my ride. I'd told Kailyn to stay out of mine and Kadence's life. But, after all that, I couldn't believe she'd stayed at the hospital the entire time anyway.

I clenched the bedsheets, feeling angry. But I wasn't sure if I was mad because she'd stayed, or upset that I almost lost my life because she'd hidden her past from me.

"Korbin?" Kailyn said cautiously as she neared my bed.

My eyes began to focus and she looked drained. Her skin was pale, and dark circles lined her tired eyes. I could tell she'd been through a lot. She looked down at her hands and fidgeted with a Kleenex.

Digging my heels into the mattress, I tried moving myself up in the bed. "Kailyn."

She smiled. "I'm so glad you're okay." She shifted her eyes toward the door then back at me. "Kadence and your parents are on their way up. They'll be excited to see you're awake."

I forced a half smile. "Thank you for keeping her safe."

No matter how mad I was at Kailyn, I was thankful she had reacted to look out for her after my accident.

She grabbed my hand. "Of course."

As I looked into her eyes, I debated on whether or not to jerk away, but a part of me found comfort in her being there.

Memories from things I'd heard while in the coma rushed back to me. Although they were in bits and pieces, I remembered Kailyn singing to Kadence by my bed, and Kadence telling me about pictures she'd drawn for me. I may not have remembered the details of each conversation, but I remembered the sound of her sweet voice and the fact that I wanted to respond, many times, but no matter how hard I tried, I couldn't.

"Daaaddy!" Kadence squealed as she rushed to the bed and threw her body on top of mine.

The impact of her weight on my healing ribs made me grunt in pain, but I didn't care. Feeling her in my arms again was worth every bit of it.

Pulling her closer, I tightened my arm around her and smiled. "Hey, sweetheart. I missed you so much." I inhaled deeply, thankful I was alive and able to hold my daughter in my arms again. It's scary to think how close I came to losing that.

"I was so scared, Daddy," she mumbled against my shoulder. "But I knew you were going to be okay. Kailyn said you had too much fight in your heart to leave me."

Glancing at Kailyn, I mouthed, "Thank you."

She smiled and nodded.

Just then, some of Kadence's words echoed through my mind. Fight in my heart?

Kailyn bent to pick her purse up off the floor. Her shirt dipped low enough for me to notice the scar on her chest again.

I'd been so wrapped up in my own feelings about the night of the accident, I hadn't given much thought to how she must've felt when she'd found out. She hadn't lied to me or hidden it from me on purpose. I understood why she'd wanted to wait until after the rodeo to tell me. Maybe I shouldn't have reacted so suddenly. She glanced at me, and I smiled absently at her.

Kadence sat up and grabbed my hand. "Daddy, can you

come home now?"

"Soon." I gave her hand a gentle squeeze. "Very soon."

My mom and dad immediately crowded me, followed by Max and some of my closest friends. I peeked around them, trying to see Kailyn. She gathered her things and left me with Kadence and my family.

I didn't understand the ache in my chest as she walked out the door. I was the one that had asked her to get out of my life, so why did it hurt so badly to watch her leave?

Chapter Seventeen

3 Weeks Later

SOMETHING HAD BEEN BOTHERING me since the day I'd awakened from my coma, but I had to go talk to Max since he had been the doctor on call the night of the accident.

I waited in his office until he was able to speak with me. "Hart! Man, is it good to see you up and walking around," he said as he walked in. "At least you didn't mess up that pretty face of yours too much." He laughed.

I punched him on the shoulder. "Shut it."

He threw his arms around me to give me a hug then sat on the couch across from me. "What's wrong?" His brows furrowed. "For a man who just cheated death, you sure don't look very happy."

Leaning forward, I laced my fingers in my lap. "I need to ask you a serious question. It's about the night Veronica died."

I thought back to the large scar on Kailyn's chest. The same scar I'd touched with my own fingertips. It didn't look like a scar that had been there for many years. It still looked somewhat new. Maybe a year old?

Max relaxed back into his chair and raised an eyebrow. "Okay."

"I need you to tell me the name of the person who received her heart that night."

I had a feeling I knew, but I couldn't be right. I just couldn't…

Max looked at me regretfully. "You know I can't do that. I'll lose my license."

Standing up, I paced the floor. "Please, Max. I need to know." I threw my hands out to my sides. "You just don't understand…"

He stood up and grabbed my shoulders. "Calm down."

Taking a deep breath, I pinched the bridge of my nose. "I know what I'm asking you to do is wrong, but I *need* you to do this for me. Please," I pleaded. "Look, if I guess it, will you at least tell me if I'm right?"

He remained silent, but walked to his computer and began typing.

After studying the screen for a moment, he looked at me and shook his head. He didn't even have to say anything.

My hands trembled, and I continued pacing the floor. "Is it her? It's Kailyn isn't it?" I already knew the answer, but I didn't want to believe it.

I had to be wrong. But there was something in my gut telling me it was her.

"Korbin, I…" was all I heard him say.

Grabbing my stomach, I fell back onto the chair across from his desk.

Max made his way toward me. "Whoa, Korbin. It's going to be okay."

"Oh, God." I gulped. "I knew it. Kailyn was in the other car that night. She has a scar on her chest. It all makes sense now. She received Veronica's heart the night of the accident."

The words came out of my mouth, but none of them seemed to be real. No. I didn't want to believe it. It wasn't possible. It couldn't be true.

He leaned against his desk and rubbed his chin. "I don't even know what to say. I can't imagine."

"What do I do now?" I muttered. "The woman I've fallen in love with, has my wife's heart beating in her chest."

"Damn." He rubbed the back of his neck. "Does she know where the heart came from?"

Staring at the wall, I tried to process everything. The scar. The medication I'd noticed in her bathroom. Did she know she has Veronica's heart? Surely she wouldn't keep something that big from me. Would she? Finding out she knew all along would cripple me.

Sitting upright, I placed my elbows on my knees and rested my face against my hands for a few seconds before looking back up at him. "I don't think so. She says she didn't even know about it being the same accident until she saw the date on the newspaper clippings in my room."

He gazed out the window for a long moment, then he turned back to me with his game face on. "Okay. Don't freak out. Let's just think through this."

Blinking absently at him, I wasn't sure how to think through something like this.

Upon arriving back at the ranch, I walked inside to a dark, lonely house. Kadence was staying with my mom and dad while I recovered, and I hadn't seen Kailyn since the day she'd left the hospital. She kept to her word and left like I'd asked her to. The silence was deafening, so I went out to the barn to check on the horses.

Silver bolts of lightning crackled in the distance against the orange and purple horizon. I stood in the middle of the field and threw my head back, feeling the wind against my face, inhaling deeply and welcoming the smell of fresh rain.

Memories of swinging on the front porch, laughing with my wife as we watched the rain, made me angry. Thinking of her made me feel good, but was a constant reminder she was gone and I'd never get to experience those little moments with her ever again.

The clouds burst open, and rain pummeled my skin. "Ahhh!" I yelled, trying to release some of my anger. "When is this going to get easier?" I cried through the darkness, dropping to my knees. "When?"

Everyone else saw me as the tough rodeo cowboy, but I was a coward. A coward for not being true to myself and my feelings and not allowing myself to move on. It was hard, but Kailyn didn't deserve to be strung along on my disaster of an emotional meltdown. Veronica wasn't coming back and I had to find a way to fight through the pain and continue living.

Standing up, I made my way into the barn, soaking wet, and Snowflake nudged me with his snout. "Hey, boy." I rubbed his muzzle.

"I'm sure the doctor hasn't cleared you to ride yet," a familiar voice said from behind me.

Turning toward the door, I found myself staring into the blue eyes that made my heart skip a beat. I'd only known her such a short time, but that didn't matter. My feelings for her were raw and real.

Standing there in a long, red maxi dress and heels, she took my breath away. "Kailyn? What are you doing here?"

The empty part of my heart started to come alive again.

She neared me and Snowflake. She, too, was wet, obviously having been caught in the rain, which had now subsided. "I'm sorry. I was on my way back to Leesa's after leaving a party and thought I'd stop by. I was hoping to just sneak in and out." She held a blue folder up in front of her. "I needed to drop these reports off for the next ranch manager you hire." She placed the folder on top of the large wooden table by the stalls. "I also need to get a few of my belongings out of the office." She glanced down and fidgeted with the key in her hand. "I didn't know you'd be here."

"It's okay. You can get whatever you need." My nerves bounced all over the place, making me feel like an emotional basket case.

It was a struggle to restrain myself from pulling her into my arms and telling her I never wanted to lose her again, then, I remembered finding out about the heart transplant and wondered if she knew.

"Thank you." She nodded. "I won't be long." She started to walk past me, but stopped. "You look great by the way." She stared at me, searching my eyes, internalizing something. She lurched forward, throwing her arms around me.

"I'm glad you're okay, Korbin." Then she took a step back and smiled. "I'm sorry I lied to you." She wiped a tear from the corner of her eye. "I hope one day you'll find it in your heart to forgive me."

Heart.

Her dress was low-cut, and her scar was visible. If I found out she'd known about the transplant, I'd feel like such a fool. Part of me thought maybe it'd be best if I didn't tell her and just let her go live her life, so I could live mine.

Snowflake stretched his head over the gate and nudged her with his snout multiple times. Snowflake was drawn to Kailyn. Every time she was around he would nudge her, snort, whicker, or rear up on his hind legs. As crazy as it sounded, it was as if he sensed she had Veronica's heart.

He softly laid his head on her chest and she wrapped her arms around him, closing her eyes. "Hi, Snowflake," she whispered. She glanced at me and stepped away from him. "I'm—I'm sorry, Korbin." She looked like she'd just been chastised, or was about to be.

Turning my head, I looked at Snowflake then back at Kailyn, blinking in awe of it all. "It's okay. I think you should ride him."

I swallowed hard and thought about what I'd just said.

Her eyes widened. "What?"

Maybe it was a sign. Maybe it was what I needed to let go. I'd been holding onto Snowflake because he was the last thing of Veronica's I had, and in some weird way it made me feel closer to her, but I knew it had only been holding me back. Giving me some kind of weird false hope that Veronica would somehow come back and ride him again. Even thinking it made me feel foolish and even a bit selfish.

Walking over, I grabbed a saddle off the banister. "Yeah. I think you should ride Snowflake," I replied, my voice stronger, more determined.

This needs to happen. It's the right thing to do.

"Now?" She looked toward the doors. "It's raining outside."

I led Snowflake out of the stall and saddled him. "It's okay. A little rain never hurt anyone."

Her brows furrowed, and her mouth twisted in disbelief. "Are you sure you're okay?"

I chuckled, trying to reassure myself I was doing the right thing. "I'm fine." I handed her the reins. "Please. For me?"

Deep down I knew it was now or never for me. I needed this to find some kind of peace again.

"Okay." She was apprehensive, but took the reins anyway.

Slowly walking over, she took her heels off and put her bare foot into the stirrup. I boosted her up as she threw her other leg over.

"Riding a horse in a dress probably isn't ideal." She laughed.

She bunched her dress into her hand and I helped her onto his back. Her dress spilled over the saddle and part of Snowflake's back.

Leading Snowflake out of the barn, I stopped in the middle of the field, thankful the rain had let up to a light drizzle. "You ready?"

She smiled down at me. "Are you talking to me or Snowflake?" She laughed and stroked his crest. "I don't know, Snowflake. Are you ready?" She gave him a few pats on his neck then grabbed the reins tightly in her hands. "I think we're ready."

Taking off the lead rope, I watched as they trotted off into the distance. My breath caught. She looked beautiful. Everything from her bare feet, her long red dress, and her damp, blond hair blowing across her face in the wind.

The rain picked up, but she kept riding. Snowflake looked relaxed and free. I couldn't take my eyes off Kailyn and the way she carried herself on him—as if she'd ridden horses her entire life.

She laughed as they picked up speed and galloped by me. The sound made me shiver. I knew Kailyn wasn't Veronica, but somehow seeing her up there, knowing she had Veronica's heart, was like Veronica was going for one last ride on Snowflake. I'd found solace watching them.

I glanced up at the sky. The storm clouds had completely blocked the sun as it finished its descent behind the mountains. "You should be here," I whispered, imagining the wind carrying my words straight up to Veronica. "But, I know you're never coming back. I love you and I always will, but I have to let go and move on. I'm sorry."

The rain crashed down on me, washing away some of my grief and pain. A part of my heart would always hold Veronica's memory, but the ghost of her was pulling away from me, and I knew that's what I needed. To stop holding onto false hope.

Kailyn pulled back on the reins and Snowflake came to a halt in front of me. "That was amazing!" Her eyes beamed with excitement. "Hopefully this city girl was able to ride properly." She giggled. "Thank you, Korbin."

Tears threatened my eyes, but I held them back. "You did a great job. Snowflake really likes you." I smiled back up at her. "And you're welcome."

"Now I'm soaked. The rain is really coming down." She wiped her hair out of her eyes. "Time to get going."

Walking to her side, I reached up to help her down. Her hair clung to her face and her red dress hugged her body so perfectly against her porcelain skin. I grabbed her around the waist. She slid slowly down my body—her eyes never leaving mine.

"Ask me to stay," she whispered, catching me off guard.

"What?" I murmured.

"I know you told me you didn't want me in your life anymore, and if that's what you still want, then you'll never hear from me again." She blinked up at me as raindrops rolled down her face. "Ask me to stay. Tell me it isn't too late for us. Give us another chance. A fresh start. A clean slate."

I blinked down at her and held her face in my hands. "I was upset about you lying to me, but it wasn't even about that. I was using that as an excuse. It's not your fault Veronica died that night. I know that now." I caressed her cheek with my thumb. "I was wrong to blame you for having anything to do with her death. I'm sorry."

Glancing down at her rain-slickened skin, I traced the top of the scar just above her neckline.

Emotion caught in my throat as I tried to speak. "I want a clean slate, too, which is why I have to tell you something." It was hard to find the right words to say.

She tilted her head, her eyes laced with confusion. "Okay..."

Taking a deep breath, I cleared my throat and continued, "The night of the accident..." I paused and blew out a breath, holding back tears. "Veronica was an organ donor." I sucked in a breath then blurted, "You were the one who received her heart that night, Kailyn."

She reached up to cover the scar with her hand and backed away slowly. Her eyes and mouth widened. She was just as shocked as I was. She didn't already know.

"I'm sorry. I need to go," she whispered. She turned in a daze and started to walk back to her car.

I reached out to grab her arm and spun her around. "Kailyn, wait. Please." Lightning lit up the sky and thunder resonated in the distance. I was soaked head-to-toe and rain poured down my face. "Dammit, Kailyn. I love you!" I yelled, surprising myself.

She gawked at me for a moment in complete shock.

I shrugged. "I know I'm broken, stubborn, and probably the most complicated man you've ever met, so I'd understand if you decide you don't want anything to do with me. But I don't think it's too late for us."

Her chest rose and fell rapidly with each quickened breath.

I rubbed the back of my neck and closed my eyes briefly to gather myself.

"True love is about knowing when to walk away and when to fight for it. And right now, Kailyn, I'm fighting like hell for it. For you. For us," I said, feeling more passionate about my decision than I'd felt in a very long time. I threw my arms out to my sides. "Here I am, with open arms, ready to fight for a love I believe in."

With each flash of lightning, I could see the confusion in her gaze. I'd thrown so much at her all at once. It was no wonder she was conflicted. Why can't anything just be easy with her?

She stepped closer and pushed me several times, anger flashing across her face. "You can't tell me you want me out of your life, tell me your wife's heart is beating in my chest, and then tell me you love me!" she cried. "Why? Why would you do this? Why is this happening?" she sobbed. "Do you really love me, Korbin? Or did you only say it because you don't want to move on from your wife and I have her heart?" She narrowed her eyes at me. The words stung like a blow to the chest, making it hard to breathe. "I'm not her. I'll never be her, and I'll never replace her. I don't want to."

I took a breath and nodded, just letting the rain wash down my face, over my body. "I know you're not, Kailyn and I'm not asking you to!" I yelled over the howling winds and claps of thunder. "I fell in love with you before I even found out about the transplant. I was just too afraid to tell you." I paused, letting her absorb. It was more like I was too afraid to admit it to myself. "I love you because of the person you are. I tried not to fall in love with you, especially so quickly, but it happened and I'm *not* sorry for that." I grabbed her arms and wanted so badly to get through to her. "I was a coward. I thought by cutting ties with you, my love for you would go away, too. I wasn't thinking about anyone but myself." I brushed the wet hair from her face. "While I was in the hospital you took care of Kadence and the ranch all while never leaving my side. I can never repay you for what you've done for us."

She shook her head and her eyes softened. "I don't expect anything in return, Korbin. I've done everything out of love. Nothing more."

"You wanted me to ask you to stay." I stepped back and held my hand out to her. "This is me begging you not to go.

180

Clean slate." In one last effort to get her to stay I added, "No more lies, no more running away, just you and me, moving forward and creating a fresh start toward becoming a family. It's not gonna be easy, Kailyn, but I feel in my heart it'll be worth it."

She blinked the rain from her eyes, each drop cascading down her face and shoulders. "I'm sorry, Korbin. I thought I could, but I can't." She pointed to her scar. "This changes everything." I stepped closer to her and she raised her hand to stop me. "After your accident, I thought I'd lost you forever. My entire world was turned up-side down that day. For weeks I sat by your hospital bed and blamed myself. I can't go through that heartbreak again if you decide later you want me out of your life again." She shook her head. "Honestly, there are no pieces of my heart left to break. I think we just both need some time to let everything soak in before we try this."

She looked wilted, defeated, and heartbroken.

Feeling defeated myself, I wished there was something I could say or do to make her change her mind. Maybe she was right, though. Maybe we both needed some time to process everything before moving forward.

Standing helplessly in the pouring rain, I watched her walk away. I thought about stopping her, again, but I didn't. Why would I? As badly as I wanted her, I had to let her go— let her leave. It was the right thing to do…or was it? I wasn't really sure what the right thing to do was anymore. My life had been so simple before she came into the picture, but I didn't want to go back to the man I was before she came along. She'd changed me and made me feel alive again. She brought me closer to my daughter and also taught me there are things in this world worth fighting for again.

As I watched her drive away, I found comfort in knowing I didn't regret opening my heart and finding love again, no matter what the outcome would be.

Kailyn

After nearing the end of the long driveway, I stopped, gripping the steering wheel so tightly my fingers burned. Why was I so conflicted? I wanted to leave, keep my dignity and heart intact, but I also wanted to turn around, run into his arms, and believe everything would be fine. How did my life get so overly complicated so quickly?

Pressing a hand to the scar on my chest, I sobbed. I couldn't believe this was happening. Was this some kind of cruel joke? My move to Montana was supposed to be relaxing—a fresh start. Not one blow after another while dealing with earth-shattering discoveries about how messed up my life truly was.

I wasn't convinced Korbin was completely ready to move on and truly love again, not—without limitations. Or that he'd only said he loved me because his late wife's heart was beating in my chest. I'd longed to hear those words leave Korbin's lips, but maybe it was too late. Maybe I would never be able to fully enjoy our time together without the constant fear that he didn't really love me for me. One thing was for sure. I had to make sure we both were fully committed before taking that step, because Kadence was involved. Her heart didn't deserve to be broken again. She'd been through too much already.

Taking one last glance behind me through my rearview mirror, I pulled onto the open road and suddenly realized I'd never gotten what I needed from the office because of my surprising interaction with Korbin. It would have to wait. I wasn't going back now and I wasn't sure if I ever would.

Chapter Eighteen

Kailyn

"**G**OOD MORNING, SUNSHINE," LEESA crooned as she opened the curtains, scorching my retinas with the bright sunshine.

Turning my back to her, I pulled the pillow over my head. "Ugghh" I groaned.

"Oh, no you don't." She yanked the pillow off. "You're not gonna stay in bed all day feeling sorry for yourself or for Korbin. It's been a week and I'm pretty sure you're still in the same pajama's you were in last weekend." She clapped her hands together. "You're gonna get out with me today, and we're gonna have some fun girl time."

There was no fighting with her. She'd always win. "Fine." I flung the blanket off and forced my body to move.

I hadn't told Leesa about the heart transplant yet, and I wasn't sure if I would ever tell anyone to be honest. Even though she was my best friend, I wanted to keep that between

Korbin and me for now.

We entered the small, down-town area and Leesa pulled into a parking spot on Main Street. "We're gonna stop by Deb's Diner to grab some lunch. "I'm starving."

Inside Deb's, we took a seat by the window. A waitress with dark, curly hair and hazel eyes approached our table and set two coffee cups and two glasses of water down in front of us. "Hi, Leesa." She smiled. "Nice of you to bring Kailyn in with you today."

I looked at her nametag pinned to her orange V-neck. "Jamie," I said, trying to figure out how she knew who I was. "Do I know you?"

She tilted her head and pushed her thin-rimmed glasses up the bridge of her nose. "It's a small town, honey. This isn't New York. I know everyone in Whitefish."

That's right. Even after a few months living here, it was still hard to remember news traveled fast in small towns and everyone knows everyone.

She poured coffee in each cup. "How are yinz doing today?"

I raised an eyebrow. "Yinz?"

Leesa chuckled. "Jamie here is originally from the Pittsburgh area." She nodded. "She moved here about ten years ago, but a part of Pittsburgh remains with her." She looked up at Jamie and smiled. "We're doing great, thanks."

"That's good. What can I get'cha?"

I glanced down at the menu. "What's good here?"

"Deb is known for her homemade lasagna. It's my favorite." She pointed at the sandwich part of the menu. "Or, if you want something lite, her BLTs are out of this world. She uses bacon from her own farm and all veggies she uses here are from her own garden or from local farms. She paused and pointed to a photo up on the wall. "Like Korbin's."

Glancing up on the wall behind me, I saw a photo of Korbin smiling in front of the diner while holding a large basket of vegetables. *Great. Korbin's everywhere in this town.*

I sighed. "I'll have the BLT with fries, please," I said, forcing myself to order something. With everything going on between Korbin and me, and no longer having a job, I hadn't felt like eating much lately.

The waitress turned to Leesa. "And you? The usual?"

"No, I think I'm gonna mix it up a bit this time." She eyed the menu. "I'll have the deluxe cheeseburger with cheese fries and a large coke with extra ice." She handed the menu back to Jamie. "Oh, and a large chocolate milkshake."

My eyes widened.

"What?" She shrugged. "I'm hungry. That's what happens when you're eating for two. These cravings are out of control." She smiled coyly.

I gasped. "Wait! What? Eating for two? Cravings?"

"Yep. That's right. I'm pregnant!" She squealed, waving her hands frantically. "We just found out and couldn't wait to tell you."

I leapt forward, over the table, to give her a hug. "I'm so happy for you guys. I'm gonna be an aunt!" I touched my hand to her belly. "Aunt Kailyn is gonna spoil you like crazy, little one."

Laughing, I sat back down and sighed. The news of my

little niece or nephew was just what I needed to help boost my spirits.

"Thank you," Leesa said, still beaming. "We're so excited. You're the first one I've told."

Jamie reached out and touched Leesa's shoulder. "Well, congratulations, Lee. That's wonderful news." She looked over at me. "Would you like anything for dessert?" She pointed at a cake on the counter. "The red velvet cake here is to die for."

I shrugged. "Sure, why not? If I don't eat it, I'll just pass it along to her," I said, smirking at Leesa.

She kicked me under the table. "Hey, now. Watch it!"

We all laughed and for a moment I was truly enjoying myself and had forgotten about the drama with Korbin. It was nice laughing again.

"Okay." She took the menus from us. "I'll get this put in for ya and bring your milkshake and coke shortly."

She walked away and disappeared into the kitchen.

Reaching across the table, I grabbed Leesa's hand. "Wow. A baby?" *My best friend is going to be a mother.* "I can't believe you're gonna be a mom."

"You can't believe it?" Her eyes widened. "I can't believe it either." She took a sip of her water. "I never thought I'd actually want to have kids, and I didn't until I met Jake." She grinned at the mention of his name.

I smiled at her. "You deserve all the happiness in the world."

Her brows furrowed and she leaned across the table. "So do you, Kailyn."

The waitress returned and placed our drinks on the table in front of us. "Your food will be out shortly. Let me know if I can get you anything else."

Unwrapping my straw, I placed it into my water. "Thank you, Jamie."

"You're welcome." She smiled. "I'll be back with your food soon."

Leesa placed a finger on her straw and stirred her drink with it. "So, are you gonna tell me what happened with Korbin that night?"

I took a sip of my water then said, "He told me he loved me".

I still wasn't ready to tell her the biggest part, that I had Veronica's heart. I wanted to, but I wasn't sure how she would react. Besides, I really didn't want to bring up such a heavy subject to take away from her big news.

Her mouth dropped open slightly. "That's a huge change from him wanting you out of his life for good."

"Yes, I know." I groaned. "The hardest part is leaving Kadence behind."

I'd gotten so attached to Kadence and really bonded with her in such a short time. I hated she was caught in the middle of our issues.

Leesa smiled softly. "You have a very kind heart, Kailyn. You're gonna get your happily ever after, whether it's with Korbin or someone else."

She had no idea just how true that was. I'd have to tell her about receiving Veronica's heart when the time was right.

"Thanks, LeeLee. I love you." I smiled back at her.

Jamie returned and placed our plates down in front of us. "Here you go, ladies."

It was nice having lunch and laughing with Leesa like old times. I'd forgotten what it felt like to laugh. The past few weeks had been one hell of an emotional roller coaster.

Suddenly, a loud shriek came from across the diner. "Kailyn!" I glanced up and saw Kadence running toward me. She pounced into my arms and squeezed me in a giant hug. "I've missed you so much." She frowned. "Where have you been?"

Korbin walked up behind her. I was so taken aback by seeing Kadence that I barely noticed him. "Kadence, let's not interrupt her. She's having lunch." He tipped his hat at Leesa then at me. When his tired eyes stopped on mine, his gaze carried a sadness that made me frown. "Sorry about that, ladies," he said, breaking our eye contact.

"No, it's okay," I said reassuringly.

I smiled at Kadence as she bounced with excitement.

"When are you coming back to the ranch?" she asked with a hopeful gaze.

I looked up at Korbin then back at Kadence. "I'm not sure, sweetie. I have some stuff going on right now that I need to take care of." I gulped. I hated lying to her. I just wanted everything to work out, so I could be a constant part of her life.

"Well, I hope you come back soon." She dropped her head. "I really do miss you."

I touched her shoulder. "I miss you, too."

My heart was torn in two and I wanted to move back to the ranch and pretend none of this had ever happened. Just go back to Korbin being my boss and me running the ranch. At least then Kadence would be a part of my life in some way.

"Come on, Kadence," Korbin prompted. He tipped his hat again at both of us. "It was great seeing you ladies."

Leesa smiled. "You, too."

I forced a small smile and blinked the stinging tears from my eyes. "You, too," I said, my voice hitching.

Korbin turned to walk away, and Kadence quickly leaned in and whispered, "Daddy really misses you, too. He's been so sad lately. Please come home soon." With one more squeeze, she bounced off my lap and quickly ran to their table.

"Come home," I whispered, echoing her words.

The ranch had been my home while I worked there. I loved living on the ranch, and I'd be lying if I said I didn't miss it—and them.

"I know that look," Leesa said, breaking me from my thoughts.

"What look?"

"The, *I'm thinking too much instead of just following my heart* look." She raised an eyebrow. "You love them both, Kailyn. Why not just give it one last shot?"

I sighed and shoved a fry in my mouth. "Because. Things are just…complicated. I can't get close to them and risk losing them again."

She placed her hand on mine. "Love is the most beautiful, yet vicious, emotion we can experience. It can lift you up or tear you apart." She took a gulp of her soda. "However, the fact that you're so unhappy right now should tell you how much you'd rather try to make it work with Korbin than waste the rest of your life being miserable and wondering *'what if'.*" She nodded her head in Korbin's direction and smiled. "Trust me. It's worth the risk."

Glancing over at their table, I sighed. Leesa did have a point. I was miserable without them.

Kadence threw a fry into the air and tried to catch it in her mouth. Korbin laughed and tried two fries just to show her up, but he missed and they toppled into his lap. He'd do anything to make her happy.

Kadence's laugh made me giggle.

"See," Leesa said. "Why don't you just ask Korbin to sit down and talk through things?" she asked. "After your last conversation, you already know how he feels."

As if he felt me watching him, Korbin's gaze met mine from across the room. He gave me a half grin and nodded before turning his attention back to Kadence. I wanted to listen to Leesa. I really did, but...

"It's more complicated than that." I picked my glass of water up and took another drink before setting it back down on the table. "I've spent most of my adult life chasing men who only hurt me in the end. I don't think my heart can take much more." I took a bite of my sandwich and stared absently out of the window. "Besides, how do I know he won't ask me to leave again when things get tough?" I turned back to her.

"He asked you to leave before his accident, Kailyn. In a fit of anger," she pointed out. "You know people say things they don't mean sometimes when they're angry." She took a sip of her thick milkshake and narrowed her eyes at me. "It's obvious to everyone—but you apparently—that he's really in love with you. There's no denying that. Besides, you know how stubborn cowboys can be." She smirked. "Just follow your heart and tell your mind to shut up."

I laughed. "Maybe you're right, but my heart is what's gotten me in this situation to begin with." There was a double meaning behind those words—only she had no clue.

KORBIN

The last person I wanted to run into was Kailyn. After the way we'd left things a week ago, I wasn't sure how to come back from that. I glanced at Kadence and wondered how she'd react to the news if she found out that her mother's heart was beating inside Kailyn's chest. Should I tell her? Should I not? A million questions whipped around in my head violently as I tried to make sense of everything.

"Daddy," Kadence said, dipping another fry in her ketchup. "When is Kailyn coming back home?"

I smiled at her. "Honey, our home isn't actually Kailyn's home. She was just staying there to help me at the ranch."

I wasn't sure if I was trying to convince her of that or myself.

She frowned. "But…I really like Kailyn—a lot. She's my friend. I did what she told me to do at school and now the bully doesn't bother me anymore." She smiled. "She's also really good at cooking, dancing, and braiding my hair," she added, shoving another fry in her mouth.

"Easy, Kadence. You're gonna choke." I chuckled.

Flashes of Kailyn dancing in the kitchen with Kadence filled my mind and then more memories of our dancing together at the bar. I couldn't argue Kadence's logic. She was oblivious to the much bigger problems at hand, so it was hard for her to understand my decisions.

I looked over and noticed Kailyn and Leesa walking toward our table. "Kailyn!" Kadence yelled. "You wanna join us for dessert?" She looked at me for permission, her eyes beaming with excitement.

I cleared my throat and shook my head. "Honey, I'm sure Kailyn has other things to do."

"Come on…pleeease?" Kadence begged, her light-brown eyes imploring.

"Oh, she's pulling out the puppy dog eyes," Leesa laughed. "How do you say no to that?"

I nodded at Kailyn in a shared understanding. Kadence had been through a lot and I didn't want to disappoint her.

"Okay, maybe I'll stay. Just for a few minutes." She slid into the booth beside Kadence. "But only if we order chocolate cake," she added with a special smile for my daughter, making my heart melt. She was great with her.

Kadence giggled. "Of course, is there any other kind of cake?"

Leesa leaned over to Kailyn. "Call me when you're done if you need a ride home."

"Okay, will do. I'll probably just take the town cab."

She smiled. "Well, if you need me to get you I can. It's not like we live far." To me, she said, "It was nice seeing you, Korbin, and you, too, Princess Kadence."

I tipped my hat. "You, too."

After she left, we sat there awkwardly for a second with just Kadence's chatter to fill the silence. Finally, our waitress brought out the biggest piece of chocolate cake I'd ever seen.

She winked at Kadence. "I put an extra-large scoop of ice cream on there and extra cherries. Just how you like it."

Kadence and Kailyn practically dug in before the waitress had even set the plate on the table. I reached to get a bite myself and Kadence clinked her spoon with mine.

"Hey!" I said. "This cake is big enough to feed an army. I think you can share a little…"

"A small army maybe," Kadence responded with *little girl* attitude.

Kadence turned to Kailyn. "Daddy's taking me to ride Midnight after this. You wanna come ride with us?"

"Ummm," Kailyn stammered, looking up at me.

"Pleeease, Daddy?" she pleaded, also looking up at me.

I wanted more than anything to spend the day with them both, but I wasn't sure where Kailyn and I stood yet. "If Kailyn wants to come, she's more than welcome to," I said carefully.

Kadence clapped. "Yay!"

Kailyn stared blankly at me from across the table then smiled at Kadence. "Okay, then." She shrugged. "I guess we're going horseback riding."

Chapter Nineteen

W E RODE THE TRAILS on the ranch for hours, heading back home as the sun set. Kadence was tired and decided to ride with me on Champion on the way back, so I put her in front of me and tied her horse's reins to Champion's stirrup so he wouldn't decide to run off on us in the dark.

"Snowflake was mommy's horse," Kadence said as we trotted through the winding trails. "She'd be really happy that someone is riding him again and keeping him healthy." She yawned.

I was afraid Kadence would've been upset about Kailyn riding Snowflake, but surprisingly, she was excited to see him out and trotting again. It didn't seem to bother her.

"Someone's tired." I laughed, glancing down at her as she slumped over onto Champion's neck and fell asleep. Her long hair draped over half of her face and the rest of it spilled out over Champion's mane.

"The ride tired her out." Kailyn laughed softly as we trotted into the barn. "How does she even sleep like that?"

"You'd be surprised at some of the ways she can sleep," I chuckled. "This girl belongs on a horse. Doesn't surprise me she can sleep on one."

After bringing Champion to a halt in front of his stall, I carefully dismounted and carried Kadence inside to bed. Tucking her in, I kissed her forehead then turned the lamp off by her bed before heading back out to the barn.

Kailyn had already taken the saddles off each of the horses and was putting them back in their stalls.

"You don't have to do that. I can take care of it." I wanted to wrap my arms around her again and hug her to my chest.

She shrugged and locked Snowflake's stall door. "I don't mind. It actually kind of feels nice being back here at the ranch."

She rubbed her hands against her jeans and we both stood in silence just staring into each other's eyes. Her gaze was soft, but fierce. Even from fifteen feet away, the chemistry between us was still there. My entire body ached to be near her again.

"Will you stay?" I asked, my heart beating like a race horse in my chest. "I don't like the way we left things before. I'd really like it if you'd stay and try to figure this all out."

She glanced down at the ground then back up at me. "Sure."

Kailyn

Korbin started a fire outside in the fire pit and repositioned some of the logs with the fire poker. The embers glowed, illuminating his strong jaw. The dry wood sizzled and popped under the heat and the musky smell filled my nose. A blanket of stars twinkled overhead and a chill in the air made me shiver.

It was quiet, other than the crickets serenading us from the creek below. We were both quiet. Neither of us knew how to start the conversation.

Inhaling deeply, I relaxed and stared at the creek. Water trickled over the rocks, and the moon cast shadows of trees as they rippled through the water. I'd never been able to experience such serenity while living in the city.

I broke the silence. "I'm sorry."

Korbin stared absently into the fire. "For what?"

"For everything." I moved closer to him and sat down on the log beside him. "For ruining your life. For not telling you right away when I found out what happened that night. I'm just sorry for all of it," I said softly, that night still haunting me.

He picked a stick up and threw it into the fire. "You didn't ruin my life, Kailyn." He sighed. "If anything, you've saved me from myself." He turned his attention to me, the reflection of the nearby flames dancing in his eyes under the brim of his cowboy hat. "I swear when I'm with you my mind is a jumbled mess. It's like a rainstorm in my head. Thoughts of what I should've said or should've done the last time we were together."

The words he spoke were raw and honest. I knew he was

laying everything out on the table and wasn't holding anything back. *Maybe we should give it one last shot.* Since everything was out in the open and there were no more secrets, we could start over.

I leaned in closer, needing to feel him near me. "Well, we're here now. Just tell me. No regrets."

He ran his fingers through my hair. "You showed me it's possible to love again and to feel it in return. I owe it to myself and Kadence to give us a chance and see where this goes." He closed his eyes and clinched his jaw for a moment then relaxed as he continued, "Nothing about our future is certain, but one thing I am sure of is my love for you." My breath hitched and I wanted to kiss him so badly. "I'm tangled up in love with you, Kailyn."

He took a deep breath. "I've waited for so long to feel this way again. To feel anything again." Glancing back at the fire, he shook his head. "I've spent the last year telling myself I'd always be a single father and could never open my heart to another woman." He turned and searched my eyes. "Then you came along."

I squeezed my eyes shut for a moment to keep tears from falling.

He frowned. "When I told you I wanted you out of my life that day, I was so angry with you and didn't know how to process it." I remembered the anger he spoke of. That night, when he looked at me, his eyes were smoldering like embers ready to blaze. "I was hurt, shocked, and immediately raised the guard back up over my heart to protect myself, and Kadence, from another heartbreak."

Wiping tears from my eyes, I finally found my voice. "I'd never in a million years have thought I'd be sitting here in

Whitefish, Montana, in love with a cowboy, wearing muddy cowgirl boots." We both laughed. "I'm not perfect, and I've made some mistakes, I know that, but I don't want us to live the rest of our lives together constantly saying *I'm sorry*." I rubbed his thigh. "If we move forward, we have to put this behind us and not dwell on the past, or it'll set us up for failure in the future."

"I agree." He nodded. "I want you to know my feelings for you have nothing to do with me finding out you received Veronica's heart. I fell in love with you before I found out about the accident or that you received the transplant." He inhaled a deep, steadying breath. "I in no way blame you for what happened that night." His gaze softened and I knew he was telling the truth. "Yes, decisions could've been made to avoid what happened, but none of what happened was your fault."

Grabbing a large stick, he poked some of the logs in the fire to reposition them. "I've been dealing with my own demons and blaming myself for so long. I should've been able to do something to save her, but I couldn't."

He paused as if his mind had wandered back to that night.

A frown touched his lips, "We'd just left the bar where I played a set with Max and the band. We were on our way home." He shook his head. "I just thank God Kadence wasn't with us that night."

I sighed, not really knowing how to take his pain away. "None of this is gonna be easy—but it's gonna be worth it." Taking his cowboy hat off, I placed it on the log beside of me and rested my hand against his cheek. "We only have two choices here. We can cut ties forever and move on, *for good*, or we can learn from everything and choose to be happy and move forward."

He took my hand in his and kissed it, causing me to pause for a moment to gather my thoughts. "I feel like this is meant to be, Korbin. I know it sounds crazy, and I'm sure we'll be the talk of the town when they find out what happened, but this feels right. Being with you and Kadence just feels right. I can't explain it."

His brows furrowed. "I don't care what anyone thinks." He placed his hand under my chin. "You, me, and Kadence are all that matters right now. Nobody else even needs to know you received Veronica's heart that night. Let's just concentrate on us for now."

"You have my mommy's heart, Kailyn?" a soft whisper came from behind us.

We both jumped up and my heart sank to my stomach. I knew we'd have to tell her eventually, but I didn't want her to find out like this.

She rubbed the sleep from her eyes and stepped closer to us by the fire.

Bending down in front of her, I looked up at Korbin for help. His eyes were wide and mouth slightly opened as if he wanted to say something, but couldn't find the words.

He cleared his throat and bent down in front of her, rubbing her arms. "Yes, sweetheart. Do you remember when we talked after mommy died about how she saved other people's lives like a real superhero?"

She slowly nodded her head, *yes*.

He glanced at me and back to Kadence. "Well, she donated her organs to help other people live." Emotion caught in his throat and he swallowed back the tears. "Kailyn was one of those people. She got your mommy's heart."

Tears welled in her eyes. She took a breath and tried to process the news. She looked at Korbin then back at me. I was expecting her to hate me, scream at me, cry, or to run off and never want anything to do with me again. I was prepared for the worst.

Tears slid down her cheeks. "Don't you see, Daddy?" Her eyes widened. "Mommy sent Kailyn to watch over us." She looked at me then back at Korbin. "She promised me I'd never be alone if anything ever happened to her. That she'd always be with me." She shook her head matter-of-factly. "Mommy never broke a promise, Daddy." She sniffled, and a smile spread across her lips. "She sent Kailyn here to take care of us."

Without warning she threw her arms around my neck and squeezed. "Thank you, Kailyn. Thank you for loving me and my daddy." I inhaled sharply as she broke the hug and traced part of the scar on my chest with her tiny fingers. "My mommy had the best heart in the world. Now, you do," she whispered.

My throat and chest tightened. I couldn't breathe. I tried to take in air, but I just couldn't. Her words touched me in ways I never imagined. I hadn't expected her to react this way about the news, and by the look on Korbin's face, neither had he.

Korbin grabbed Kadence by the arms and pulled her into him. He squeezed her tightly and rubbed the back of her head with his hand. I fell back onto the ground and sat there in disbelief, watching him hold his daughter as her words continued to rip through my head. *My mommy had the best heart in the world. Now, you do.*

The way she viewed the entire situation baffled me. She was only a kid, but she seemed to accept the situation much better than we did.

After that, Korbin took Kadence inside to talk with her in private. He looked at me over his shoulder. "I'll be right back."

Giving them the space they needed, I turned to face the fire and watched the flames dance in the wind as I sat on the cold, hard ground in silence, taking it all in.

Pulling my knees to my chest, I sobbed. Each tear that fell carried with it weeks of pent up emotions. I cried for me, for Kadence, for Korbin, and even for Veronica. She'd had such an amazing husband and daughter. It didn't seem fair she wasn't here to enjoy them. So, I cried alone, in the dark, as the fiery glow faded to ash in front of me.

After gathering myself, I walked inside to call a taxi. I wanted to give Korbin time alone with Kadence.

"Kailyn?" Korbin called from behind me. I turned to find him slowly descending the stairs. He tilted his head and glanced at the front door then back at me. "Are you leaving?"

Placing my phone on the table by the door, I walked toward him. "I was going to. You were gone for a while, and I thought maybe you needed this extra time tonight with Kadence." I met him at the bottom of the stairs. "That's a lot for a kid to process." I shrugged and shook my head. "Hell, that's a lot for anyone to process."

"I love that you'd do that for us, but I was actually coming back down because Kadence wants to know if you'd tuck her back in bed." He extended his hand. "But I understand if you don't feel up to it."

Searching his eyes, I tried to figure out how he felt about

that request, but his facial expression was indifferent. "I'm sorry she found out like this." I thought for a moment about how it seemed I'd done nothing but mess up their lives in one way or another since the day I'd arrived.

His eyes widened slightly. "Honestly, I'm relieved." He sighed. "Now she knows and we can all move forward."

"Yes, move forward." I grabbed his hand. "I really like that idea."

Walking upstairs, I stood in front of Kadence's room and knocked. The door was cracked open, spilling light from her lamp into the hallway. "Can I come in?" I asked wearily, still half expecting her to lash out at me at some point. I wasn't sure why it was so hard for me to accept she was okay with everything.

She yawned. "Come in." The room was dark except for the small, polka-dot lamp on the bedside table. Leaning over, I grabbed the blanket and pulled it up to just under her chin.

She blinked slowly, her eyelids heavy. "Can you lay with me?"

I hesitated for a moment then nodded. "Sure."

She scooted over just enough for me to lay beside her, then she threw her arm over my stomach and laid her head against my chest. My heart raced. "That's my mommy's heart beating in there?"

Biting my lip, I squeezed my eyes closed to steady my emotions. "Yes."

"I can hear it," she whispered.

Sitting up, I gently pulled her up with me. "Kadence, honey. You know that I'm me, Kailyn. And I'd never try to replace your mom." She blinked up at me. "No one can ever love you as much as your mom and dad do, but I'd like to be a part of your and your dad's life, if you're okay with that?"

She nodded and yawned again. "I love you, Kailyn," was all she said. Four simple words that meant the world to me.

Overwhelmed by her words, I rubbed the back of her head and hugged her tightly.

She nestled back down under the covers, curled up against my side, and I rubbed her head lightly as the sound of my beating heart lulled her to sleep. I wasn't sure where we'd go from here, but I knew I'd do whatever it took to make sure we'd all go there together.

Chapter Twenty

KORBIN

S TANDING IN THE SHADOWS, I watched the interaction between Kailyn and Kadence. The hardest thing I'd ever had to do was to look into my baby girl's eyes and tell her that her mom died.

I'd blamed myself for a long time. Veronica didn't want to go out that night. She was tired and begged me to stay home, but I insisted she come out to hear us play. I squeezed my eyes shut as I relived that night all over again. Veronica screaming, tires screeching, glass shattering, me reaching out to ask if she was okay with no response. If I had only known that night would've been the last night I'd have with her...

After my parents arrived at the hospital, I had to deliver the news to Kadence that she no longer had a mother. I'd never forget the confusion, anger, and sadness in her eyes that night. I kissed every tear that ran down her cheeks and it killed me to see her hurting so badly. I knew Kailyn wasn't

Veronica, but Kailyn was mending Kadence's heart, and mine, in ways I never would've imagined. Whether it was fate, or a coincidence, I had to believe she was sent to us for a reason.

Walking down the hall, I went to get ready for bed. I was mentally and physically exhausted and needed to sleep.

After turning some music on, I turned the shower on as hot as it would go and stepped inside. Placing my hands up on the cold tile in front of me, I let the water run over my head and down my neck and shoulders. Thinking back, I remembered the day I'd first met Kailyn and how desperate I'd been for help with the ranch and with Kadence.

I stilled as the shower door opened and a pair of hands wrapped around my stomach and chest. "Kailyn," I breathed. My pulse quickened and my body stirred beneath her touch.

She pressed her cheek to my back. "I really need to be near you right now. Is that okay?"

I placed a hand over hers. "Of course."

Turning to face her, I grabbed her face in my hands and gazed into her sky-blue, swollen eyes before placing a kiss on her full lips.

She grabbed my body wash off the shelf and began to lather my chest. Her touch relaxed me and took my mind off everything except for her.

She smiled, gliding her soapy fingers down my chest, looking up at me through hooded eyes. I didn't see confusion in them anymore. Instead, I saw a strong, confident woman who finally, wholeheartedly, knew what she wanted and wasn't afraid to take it.

Leaning down, I kissed each freckle on her shoulder. "I'm so glad you're here."

She grabbed my hand. "Me, too."

She flipped the bottle over and poured some of the soap into my palm. Her lips parted slightly and she exhaled. She closed her eyes as I caressed her body with the bubbles, enjoying the silky suds as they dissolved between my fingers. As my hands followed the curves of her body, she blinked up at me, her eyes locked with mine.

Wrapping my arm around her, I pulled her flush against my body, kissing her just below her ear before continuing a trail down the dip between her neck and shoulder. Everything about her seemed flawless—every scar and every freckle. She was perfect. As I kissed down her chest and over her transplant scar, she flinched, but quickly relaxed and let me continue. She tilted her head back and water splashed onto her chest, cascading over her breasts.

My breathing quickened and my heart raced. "You're so damn beautiful," I said, taking a moment to drink her in.

She grinned coyly. "Thank you, Mr. Hart. You're not too bad yourself."

Bending down, I kissed her stomach and continued down to her inner thighs. She grabbed my face and pulled me back up to her, moaning against my lips. The sound reverberated through me, making me come unhinged. In one swift motion, I turned her and pressed her back against the tile. She arched her back to push away from the coldness.

Leaning in, I bit her bottom lip playfully. One more small moan and I couldn't hold back any longer. With one hand I touched her cheek and wrapped the other one around her wet hair, pulling just enough to make her look up at me, before pressing my mouth against hers.

Her lips yielded to my tongue—her kisses urgent, yet soft and seductive as she dragged her fingers down my back.

I groaned against her lips, making her shiver and lightly grazed my fingers over the goosebumps that spread across her skin.

The only thoughts running through my mind were Kailyn and how much I loved being near her. How her touch forced me to focus on the moment and push everything else away.

She wrapped her arms around my neck and one of her legs around my waist. I didn't waste any time. While looking into her eyes, I lifted her up and entered her slowly. She threw her head back against the wall and moaned, her body tensing around me. The feel of Kailyn was different each time I was with her. This time we were starting over. She wasn't confused anymore, and I had finally learned to move on and let myself love again.

Our breathing quickened as I thrust into her over and over again. The water turned cold, making her body tense around mine again. She grabbed the back of my neck and squeezed as she found her release and mine followed shortly after.

Her body slid down mine until her feet were back on the shower floor. I leaned against the tile, both arms on either side of her head and kissed her forehead, letting my lips linger for a few extra seconds.

"You're pretty amazing, you know that?" I asked, gazing into her eyes.

She stared at me for a moment before reaching up to touch my cheek, dragging her fingertips along the few-day-old stubble that covered my chin.

Her mouth pulled up at the corners and tears started to form beneath her lashes. "I can't help but feel like meeting you, falling in love with you, has mended my deepest wounds and healed me in some way." Her touch glided down my neck and over my shoulders, stopping on my bicep.

Leaning in, I rested my forehead against hers. "Love can do crazy things sometimes," I whispered, my lips inches from hers. "Falling for you has taught me how strong love really is. I never thought I'd be happy again, but you've restored the faith I'd lost."

She shivered again, quickly rubbing her arms. "Korbin, I really don't want to ruin this perfect moment, but this water is freezing. I think we need to get out now." She laughed.

Laughing, I backed away and turned off the water. She gave me a quick kiss and stepped out of the shower to get ready for bed. After standing there for a moment, letting everything sink in, I followed behind her to do the same.

As I walked out of the bathroom, Kailyn smiled and pulled the blankets down, motioning for me to slip into bed with her.

After rubbing her cheek, I tucked a strand of hair behind her ear. "Thank you," I whispered.

She put her hand on top of mine. "For what?"

"For pulling me out of a dark place." I swallowed hard. "I've been struggling for so long, and I didn't realize just how much until you came along, giving me something to fight for again." I glanced over at a large picture on the wall of Kadence in a sundress running through the field by the barn. "I've buried myself into this ranch and Kadence instead of allowing myself time to grieve." I turned my attention back to Kailyn. "I was too stubborn to admit I needed help."

She laced her fingers with mine. "I may have been here to remind you of what's important, but you took the step yourself." She smiled. "When I moved here from New York, I never thought this would be my life. When I first met you, I never would've imagined falling in love with you. When I met Kadence, I never imagined a little girl could capture my heart like she has." She arched an eyebrow. "And you know what?" She grinned and her gaze softened. "I wouldn't change anything, because it's all led us to where we are right here, right now." She moved in closer, her lips inches from mine.

Looking into her eyes, I knew in my heart I felt the same way.

After turning the lamp off, I curled up against her body, resting my head on her chest. I sucked in a breath and tears stung my eyes as I laid there, listening to the strong, steady beat of her heart. Veronica's heart.

Chapter Twenty-One

T HE NEXT MORNING, I woke to giggling on the other side of the door. Putting my robe on, I opened the door just in time to see Korbin chasing Kadence down the hallway. Standing in the doorway, I laughed as he picked her up and slung her over his shoulder.

She squealed while kicking her feet. "Daddy! Put me down!" She laughed. "Kailyn. Heeelp meee!"

"I'm coming, Kadence!" I yelled as I took off running toward them both.

"Oh, no you don't!" Korbin laughed. He put her down and they both chased me.

"Wait. What?" I shrieked. I ran into Korbin's room and they both tackled me on the bed. "This isn't fair!" I laughed. "You're not supposed to be helping him, Kadence!"

I hadn't laughed so hard in a long time. I'd been so bogged down over the years with college, Mason, work, and recovering from the accident and heart transplant, that my life had passed me by without truly enjoying it. Back in the city, I went through the motions of every day life as a professional accountant and hardly ever had time to go out and have fun or spend time with my friends. Looking back, I really regretted following in my parents' footsteps and letting work take over my life. It felt good to let loose and laugh again.

"Okay, Kadie Bug," Korbin said. "Time to go get ready. Nana will be here to pick you up soon." He gave her a fatherly pat on the butt. "You don't wanna keep her waiting."

She froze for a second and blinked up at Korbin. "You called me Kadie Bug." Her eyes widened. "You haven't called me Kadie Bug in a long time."

His smile faded and he stilled for a moment. "Hurry up now." He pointed down the hall. "Make sure you pack enough for the week."

Beaming, she skipped through the door and down the hall into her bedroom.

Korbin grabbed the back of his neck and paced the floor. Walking over to him, I rubbed his arm. "Are you okay?"

It was hard for me to understand what he was feeling when I had no idea what was going on and had to pry information out of him.

His jaw clenched.

"What's wrong?" I asked.

"She's right." He shrugged. "Kadie Bug was the nickname Veronica and I gave her from the time we found out she was a girl because Veronica loved ladybugs. I didn't realize I hadn't called her by her nickname anymore since then." He brought a hand up to his mouth and stroked his chin. "How does a father not notice something like that?" He sat on the edge of the bed and I stood in front of him. "What am I doing to her?" He stared blankly at the wall across the room. "Am I completely failing as a father?"

Even though tears formed beneath his lids, he held them back. These stubborn cowboys and their *cowboys don't cry* mantra. I stepped closer to him and ran a hand through his short, dark hair. "Korbin, it's okay to feel what you're feeling right now."

His chin trembled slightly. "What if I screw this up? A girl needs her mother."

I didn't try to understand what Korbin was going through and what he was feeling because I couldn't even imagine. His emotions were all over the place, and I was pretty sure it was because he'd been living every day since the day she died drifting through the motions of life, not allowing himself to feel or grieve. He'd held it all in for so long that now his wall was crumbling down all around him. My heart broke for him, and there was nothing I could do to help him.

Squatting down in front of him, I rested my arms on his thighs and looked into his tired eyes. "You're doing a great job with her. She's lucky to have a father like you." I swallowed back my emotions as I continued, "I know I'm not her mother, but I'll be here for her and help you in any way I can. Not to mention, you have an entire town by your side." I laughed. "Heck, even Jamie from Deb's Diner and Vern from the Country Store downtown have your back. There's no way you're going to be doing this alone."

That comment made him smile. I only hoped I was able to get through to him and ease his fears.

Narrowing my eyes, I stood and pulled him up with me. "I'm going to walk out there and help Kadence pack her things," I said, pointing to the door. "You stay in here and let it all out. The anger, frustration, sadness, whatever you're feeling. When you're ready, come join us downstairs, okay?" I said, trying to decipher his impassive glare.

He nodded and I walked out. The door clicked shut, and I leaned against it taking a deep breath. It was tough being strong for Korbin, but that's what he needed.

After graduating high school, I started spiraling out of control, and after seeking help from a counselor, it was determined most of my problems stemmed from my anger toward my parents. She suggested I do these techniques where I shout all of my frustrations into the mirror as if I were saying it to them. After the first ten seconds, I broke down and immediately felt some relief. She explained that sometimes people hold things in for so long they reach a point where their mind gets so bogged down with negativity and anger that they either seek help or self-destruct. She taught me by learning how to express the anger and hurt I'd been harboring since childhood that I could heal and get my life back on track. She was right.

Maybe it'll work for Korbin, too.

Before I walked away, I heard a shout from the other side of the door, making me jump. I was sure it wasn't pretty, but I was glad for it. He needed to get it all out somehow. After gathering myself, I took a few more deep breaths and walked to Kadence's room on the other side of the house.

While waiting on Ella and William to arrive, we rocked on the oversize, white rocking chairs on the front porch while listening to Kadence tell knock-knock jokes.

She jumped up and narrowed her eyes as she scanned the field in the distance. "Kailyn!" She pointed to the field. "I need to show you something. Hurry! Come on." She grabbed my hand and practically dragged me down the steps.

Running ahead of me, she plucked something from the ground before turning and hiding her hand behind her back. Giggling and bouncing up and down on the balls of her feet, she looked how I'd imagined myself looking when being handed a bottle of wine after a long day. Well, before my heart transplant that is.

"Close your eyes," she said, barely able to contain her excitement.

I squeezed my eyes shut and waited.

She giggled again. "Okay, open them!"

Upon opening my eyes, she squealed and practically shoved a weed in my face.

Her cheeks dimpled as her lips curved upwards. "This is a dandelion fluff."

Korbin walked up beside of me, looking much more relaxed than before. "It's rare to see those this time of year. Usually they don't make it this far into fall."

"Exactly!" Kadence chimed in. "They say if you find one after the first day of fall, you can make a wish and it'll come true." She squeezed the stem tightly in her hands and twirled around.

Korbin lifted an eyebrow at her. "Who says that?"

She propped a hand on her hip with sass. "Everybody."

Stepping closer, she held it out to me. "Come on, Kailyn. Take it," she urged. "Make a wish and blow."

I glanced at Korbin and he shrugged. "Go ahead." The

corners of his eyes wrinkled as he smiled.

Taking the flower from her, I closed my eyes and made a wish. Before blowing the seeds into oblivion, I peeked at Kadence whose excitement couldn't be contained. She couldn't stand still.

Squatting down, I whispered to her, "Would you like to help me?"

She clapped her hands together and nodded. "Yes, please."

I held it out so we could both blow it. "Okay. On three. One, two, three."

Sucking in a breath, we both blew and the light breeze carried each seed as they floated effortlessly through the air to their new destination. As I watched them, I couldn't help but think of how life was a journey much like each one of those seeds. There were so many directions my life could've gone over the years, but somehow I ended up in Montana. I looked at Kadence and up at Korbin who both were watching the seeds as well.

I ended up here. This is my life.

Once all of the seeds were out of sight, Kadence turned to me, her eyes wide. "I can't wait to see if your wish comes true." She laced her hands together under her chin. "It has to."

Just then, Ella and William's car came up the drive.

"Nana's here," Korbin said. "Let's go, kiddo."

We walked back to the house and greeted them.

"Looking good, son." William hugged Korbin with a strong pat on the back. "Nice to see you again, Kailyn," he said, turning to give me a hug as well.

We'd really gotten to know each other during the weeks Korbin was in the hospital, and I was thankful they'd both started to trust my feelings for Korbin were real and had started to accept me being in his life.

Kadence grabbed her suitcase off the front porch. "I'm ready to go." She ran up to Korbin, giving him a kiss before turning to give me a hug. "Bye, Daddy! Bye, Kailyn!" She waved as she got into the back of the car.

Ella glanced at the car and back at us. "Well, I guess someone's excited to get going."

Korbin rolled his eyes playfully. "Only because you keep bribing her with ice cream and getting to stay up past her bedtime."

"Hey." She shrugged. "I'm Nana. It's my job to spoil her."

We all laughed as they said their goodbyes and headed for the car.

Korbin and I waved as the car disappeared down the dirt road. He put his arms around my shoulders and squeezed me against him.

He kissed the top of my head. "Thank you."

I didn't even have to ask what he was thanking me for. I already knew.

Leaning my head against his chest, I sighed. "You're welcome."

Chapter Twenty-Two

KORBIN

WE SPENT THE REST of the evening in her office gathering numbers for the crops that were harvested by Zach and the other ranch hands while I was in the hospital. Kailyn was a breath of fresh air to the Hart of Country Ranch. She'd worked so hard from the hospital room making calls, sending emails, and doing whatever else needed to be done in order to make sure things continued running smoothly. I was relieved to have her here to help with the routine of running the ranch.

She touched her ear to her shoulder then rubbed the back of her neck. She'd been staring at the computer screen for so long her muscles had become stiff.

I stood behind her and massaged her neck and shoulders. She stopped typing and relaxed against my hands. We'd both been looking at numbers and scrolling through Excel spreadsheets until the lines were starting to run together.

Turning the chair around, so she was facing me, I extended a hand. "Come on."

Her brows knitted. "Where are we going?"

I grinned. "Out."

She scowled. "We have so much work to do."

"I know, and I promise to let you get back to it soon, but we need a break." I nodded toward the door. "C'mon."

She took my hand reluctantly, and we headed out to the detached garage by the house.

"Where are we going?" she asked again.

"You'll see."

In the garage, I motioned for her to come closer.

She glanced behind me at the four-wheeler. Her eyes widened. "Oh, no, no, no." She frantically shook her head.

I pulled my cowboy hat off and hung it on a hook by the door before pulling my shirt off and shoving it into the storage compartment on the back of the four-wheeler.

Jumping on, I turned the key. "Yes."

She shook her head as the engine roared to life. "Nope."

I grinned. "Come on. It'll be fun, and I promise to be careful."

Veronica and I used to always take off on spontaneous four-wheeling trips, and I actually looked forward to doing it with Kailyn.

She gazed out the door then back at me. "It's gonna be dark soon."

"I have headlights, and flashlights are in the storage bag. It'll be fine. Come on," I said in one last attempt to get her to go.

She shifted her weight to her other foot and took a deep breath. "I've never been on one before," she confessed. She wrinkled her nose. "And it's all muddy out there."

I chuckled. "That's the fun part. Stop trying to talk yourself out of it."

She glanced out at the field then back at me. I winked at her, making her giggle. "Okay, fine," she surrendered. "But you better be careful. You have precious cargo." She crawled on the back of the four-wheeler and wrapped her hands around my stomach. "Oh, and don't get me muddy."

Pretending I didn't hear her, I revved the engine and took off through the field. "What was that?"

Mud covered our boots as I drove through a large puddle.

"Korbin!" I laughed, and she hit me on the shoulder. "Stop laughing at me."

Continuing through the field, we finally entered the woods and stopped by the creek.

"We can't go through that." Realizing what I was about to do, she clung to me even tighter. "Korbin, it's too deep."

"No, it's not," I assured her. "I travel these trails all the time. It's shallow enough right here to go through it to the other side. Just hold on."

She tensed and buried her face against my back.

I placed a hand over hers. "Do you trust me?"

She relaxed and exhaled, turning her head so her cheek rested on my shoulder. "Yes."

After calming some of her fears, I took off through the water, soaking us both. She squealed, and I was pretty sure she was going to end up killing me once we returned to the house.

After we got to the other side, I stopped the four-wheeler and turned around to check on her, expecting her to be terrified. But she was smiling.

"That was so much fun!" A challenging grin spread across her lips. "Again."

I chuckled. Her determination was sexy. She'd flipped from timid to courageous in only a matter of minutes. Experiencing all of these *firsts* with her was intoxicating and affecting me more than it probably should, but I really liked it.

"You're worse than Kadence." I laughed, wiping specks of mud from her cheek. "You'll have to wait until we go back home."

We made it through the woods and to one of my favorite spots. The overlook. She gasped and gawked as the sun set behind the mountains, leaving a fiery glowing reflection on the water below us.

"Korbin," she whispered. And she didn't say anything else for a long moment. There was nothing else to say. This place was beyond words, and she felt it, too. "It's beautiful," she finally spoke.

Watching as she scanned the horizon, I remembered the first time I'd taken Veronica to this very spot. Her reaction was similar to Kailyn's. *This place is breathtakingly beautiful* Veronica said as her eyes lit up.

I turned the four-wheeler off, and she peered over my shoulder. "Wow." She sighed. "Just wow."

Kailyn

I couldn't believe what I was seeing. Being on top of that overlook made me feel like I was on top of the world. It was so peaceful. Turning my head slightly, I looked at Korbin, his face inches from mine. He peered into my eyes and leaned in, kissing me softly.

"That's not even the best part," he whispered against my lips. "Come on." He jumped off the four-wheeler, and I followed him to the edge of the woods. "Just stay on the trail. It's not far," he said as he descended the steep, rocky bank.

My heart raced and adrenaline kicked in. The closest I'd ever gotten to climbing rocks was the rock wall at my gym back in the city. I couldn't believe I was doing something so dangerous. Then again, I couldn't believe I'd attempted and done half of the things Korbin had encouraged me to do since arriving at the ranch.

He turned around to grab my hand and helped me over one last big rock. "Here we are."

"Wow." The wide stream of water rushed over the cliff and crashed against the rocks at our feet.

Being alone with Korbin surrounded by all the natural beauty of this place took my breath away.

I was so busy admiring the scenery that I hadn't noticed Korbin stripping down to his boxer-briefs next to me. "Let's go."

Without warning, he jumped into the large pool of water below.

"Are you nuts?" I scanned the area as if I was expecting someone to walk up at any moment. "No way. That water has to be freezing." I crossed my arms over my chest in defiance.

"It's not too bad." He chuckled. "You're the one who said to stop thinking so much and just enjoy life." He raised an eyebrow, challenging me.

Touché.

"That's not fair. You can't use my words against me."

Although, he did have a point.

He stood there under the waterfall, the water washing the mud from his face and running over his shoulders and abs. He grinned seductively at me, running his fingers through his hair.

"What the hell." I conceded. I pulled my shirt off, kicked my boots off, and shimmied out of my muddy jeans.

Here goes nothing.

Closing my eyes, I jumped in, the cool water taking my breath. "It's so cold." My teeth chattered.

He grinned at me roguishly. "I'll do my best to keep you warm, ma'am."

I bit my lip playfully. "I'm sure you will, cowboy."

Swimming over, he grabbed me around the waist and pulled me closer. I wrapped my legs and arms around him, surprisingly forgetting about the ice-cold water.

We drifted closer to the edge of the waterfall, mist and droplets of water spreading across my prickled skin.

He hadn't stopped smiling since we'd arrived. Glancing around, I couldn't help but wonder how many times he'd brought Veronica here. I knew I'd have to stop comparing everything we do to their relationship, but it was hard because I knew making new memories in places that held so many past memories couldn't be easy for him.

He looked at me, his face serious. "What's wrong?"

"I don't know." I glanced around again, taking it all in. "I guess I'm just thinking too much."

"About what?"

"The future," I admitted.

His brows furrowed. "What about it?"

He turned so the water ran down my back. I tightened

my arms and legs around him in response to the cold water, molding my body to his.

"What do you see?" I prodded, sucking in a sharp breath.

His body tensed, and he was silent for a moment. The only sounds that surrounded us were our bated breathing and water cascading over the rocks.

He caressed my cheek, and his body relaxed. "You," he said, confidence radiating from him. "I see you, Kailyn."

A tear slid down my cheek, and he kissed it away then lightly kissed my lips. "What about you?"

My chin trembled, mostly from the cold water but also because of my fragile emotional state. "I see you. I see us." I smiled at him. "I can't imagine my life without you and Kadence in it."

Growing up, I used to think relationships were all about status and power. Not romance and love. My parents never showed much affection toward each other, but as soon as my dad landed his next big client, he didn't waste any time whisking my mom away on a vacation to some other exotic location they hadn't been to yet.

Then, after meeting Mason, I settled. I settled for him because he'd accepted my crazy workaholic tendencies and didn't complicate my professional goals. I did care about Mason, but I wasn't head-over-heels in love with him.

Until Korbin, I didn't even know true love was real. I thought it only existed in fairy tales. Before meeting him, I'd accepted the fact that it just wasn't meant to be for me to fall in love with someone so completely that I'd have my own happily ever after.

Korbin's lips crashed down on mine, and I yielded to him as he explored my tongue with his. His kiss was demanding and seductive and it lit a fire deep within me. He pulled me out of the water and eased me onto a large, smooth rock behind the waterfall.

The sound of the rushing water crashing against the rocks heightened my senses.

His body slid against mine, and the adrenaline pulsating through my veins had me on a high I never wanted to end. I submitted to his kiss once again as he removed my panties. I wrapped my legs around him and ran my fingers through his hair, surrendering my body, my heart, and my soul to him once again.

Just before dark, we made our way back to the four-wheeler. Korbin unzipped the bag on the back of it and pulled two shirts out along with two pair of shorts.

"Here you go." He handed me one of each. "Put these on."

My hands trembled as I reached out to take the dry clothes, quickly putting them on. Even though they were baggy on me, I was thankful for some warmth and not having to put my jeans back on over my wet skin. My teeth chattered, and my body shook from the chills.

"Come on." Korbin rubbed my arms with his hands. "Let's get back and warm you up by the fire."

KORBIN

Her hands pressed against my stomach as I drove through the darkened woods back to the house. We didn't talk. There was only the roar of the four-wheeler and crunching sticks and leaves echoing through the woods.

As I navigated through the narrow trails, I thought about how much I'd changed since the day Kailyn arrived at the ranch. I was desperate for help, and she was the first one to apply who had the professional background I was looking for. Little did I know a few short months later I'd be falling in love all over again. Deep down, I knew Veronica would always have a piece of my heart, but Kailyn understood that and showed me there's room for her, as well.

Once we arrived back at the house, Kailyn stepped off the four-wheeler and glanced down at my baggy clothes that swallowed her curvy body. "I'm going to go shower and get into some of my own clothes." She laughed, holding the shorts up on her hips with one hand. "I'll meet you inside by the fire." She smiled.

After quickly showering in the mudroom in the garage, I hurried inside to start a fire then made myself a whiskey on the rocks. I set the glass on the coffee table and sat on the couch, staring into the fire, watching the flames dance back and forth.

I looked up at the photo of Veronica on the fireplace mantle, and for the first time since her death, a feeling of peace overcame me. I knew Veronica would want me to move forward with my life and be happy. She'd want Kadence to also have a strong woman in her life to help her as she grows. As much as I missed her, and as much as my heart still ached for her, I knew Kailyn had stumbled into our lives for a reason. To help me find myself again. To help me remember the important things in life and to help me strengthen my relationship with Kadence.

When Kailyn walked into the room, her shadow flickered with each ebb of the fire. She sauntered toward me in nothing but her silk robe, her damp hair draped over her neck. I drank in her beauty for a moment and couldn't move or speak. She took my breath away. Every time she entered a room, I entered this trance I couldn't pull myself out of. Not that I wanted to.

Clearing my throat, I reached over to take another drink of my whiskey before placing it back on the table.

She sat down beside of me, and I wrapped my arm around her shoulders. Her body relaxed against my side. "Thank you, she whispered."

I rested my cheek on the top of her head. "For what?"

"For today." She turned to face me. "You make me feel so powerful, like I can do anything. I want to step out of my comfort zone and try new things." She smiled seductively. "I don't know what you're doing to me, Mr. Hart, but I sure do love it."

Smiling back, I hugged her closer and nudged her neck with my nose, breathing in her skin. Hints of vanilla and honey heightened my senses as I placed a kiss on her earlobe. "Is that so?" I whispered. "I'd love to keep doing things to you."

She giggled and tilted her neck to give me access, moaning as I kissed from her ear to her shoulder. "You drive me crazy, Kailyn North. I hope you know that." I bit her neck playfully and followed it with a kiss.

She looked at me through lowered lashes and grinned.

"Darlin' you have no idea."

She crawled onto my lap and straddled me. Wrapping her arms around my neck, she ran her fingers through my hair, tugging gently.

"How is it you say it here in the country?" She scrunched her nose. "You haven't seen anything yet?"

I laughed. "You ain't seen nothing yet," I corrected her. I snaked my arms around her waist, pulling her tighter against me. "If you're gonna play the part, you have to get it right," I joked, enjoying the seductive game she was playing.

She leaned down and whispered, "Can you teach me?" Then she softly tugged on my earlobe with her teeth.

"Oh, you have no idea the things I can teach you," I drawled.

She kissed my neck just below my ear and whispered, "Show me."

As she was grinding her body against mine, I untied her robe and groaned. "Gladly."

Chapter Twenty-Three

Kailyn

"**G**OOD MORNING, SUNSHINE." KORBIN sat on the edge of the bed by my side. "You awake yet?"

I groaned and pulled the pillow over my head. "I am now."

He laughed a deep, throaty laugh and pulled the pillow off. "Come on. It's getting late."

I glanced up at the clock on the wall. "It's five-thirty in the morning," I complained. "We just went to bed like three hours ago."

"Exactly," he said matter-of-factly. "Time's a wastin'." He leaned down and whispered, "What's wrong? Did I wear you out last night?"

"Maybe." I laughed. "My entire body hurts."

He slapped me on my ass, making me squeal. "Well, we need to practice more then. You know, get your body used to it. We'll start tonight." He laughed and stood upright.

"Practice makes perfect." He started toward the door. "I'll meet you downstairs."

I wasn't really sure how that man could even function half of the time. We were up all night making love, and he was still up and dressed before five-thirty in the morning. We had gotten only three hours of sleep, max.

Throwing the blanket off, I sat up and groaned. It was going to be a long day, and I didn't think I'd be able to keep up with him. He was insatiable—and I kind of liked it...

Making my way down stairs, I overheard Korbin on the phone. Who in the world could he possibly be talking to so early in the morning?

"I don't know, man," he mumbled. "I don't think I can come back to the rodeo any time soon."

Stopping on the bottom step, my body instantly tensed, and I wasn't sure what made me angrier, the fact that he was even considering going back to the rodeo or the fact that he was talking to someone else about it instead of me.

He turned and saw me. "I've gotta go," he said quickly. "I'll call you back later." He hung up and stuck the phone in his back pocket.

He met me at the bottom of the stairs. "Good morning, beautiful," he crooned.

"Wait," I snapped. "Are you seriously considering going back to the rodeo? And so soon?" Thoughts of him flying through the air the last time he was on a bull made me shudder. "What the hell?"

"Kailyn," he started, reaching out to touch my arm.

"No." I clenched my teeth. "Don't even go there. Did you forget you spent weeks in a coma with your daughter crying at your bedside thinking you were going to die?" Fear set in again. "Why would you even consider going back?"

Not only Kadence, but I sat by his bedside every day and waited. Terrified he wouldn't pull through, and I'd never see him again. How could he want to get back to riding so quickly after staring death in the face?

His eyes narrowed. "No, I haven't forgotten."

I blinked rapidly, feeling flustered. "I sat by your bedside for weeks with your daughter and kept telling her you were going to be okay. I lied to her. I didn't really know if you were going to be or not." I threw my hands out to my sides. "I'm not going through that again, Korbin. I can't." My chest rose and fell with each quickened breath.

His gaze softened, and he began to wilt, looking sorry as if he hadn't really thought about anyone's feelings except for his own desire to go back. For a moment, I felt bad for being so hard on him. He was a grown man who could make his own decisions.

"I'm sorry." He shook his head. "You just don't understand how hard it is to give up something you're so passionate about." He shrugged. "Bull riding has been my life for so long, and a huge chunk of my income." He gestured around the house and pointed outside. "Everything I have on this ranch, I have, mainly because of my sponsorships and competition money. I've made it to the top, and that's where I've stayed for years." His brows furrowed, and the pain in his eyes hurt me deeply. "Without it, I feel lost."

He walked to the front door and gazed through the glass.

Maybe I was overreacting. In my mind, it should've been an easy decision to cut ties with the rodeo and not risk his life for any amount of money or self-fulfillment. But it wasn't that simple.

Walking up behind him, I wrapped my arms around his waist. "I'm sorry." I sighed. "There has to be some kind of a compromise," I said, grabbing his arm and turning him to face me. "I don't want you to be unhappy or resent me for not doing what you love, but I can't live in fear, wondering if the next rodeo will be your last. Kadence doesn't deserve that either."

He rubbed a hand over his face and turned, opening the door to step outside. Following him, I sat in a rocking chair behind him as he leaned against one of the front porch posts. The sunrise was just peeking over the mountains, lighting up the sky in a soft glow.

"You're right." He sighed, glancing back at me with a complacent look on his face. "I know you're right, Kailyn. I just have to figure out what path to take next."

He sat in the chair beside me and reached over, grabbing my hand. "I'm not sure why I even considered going back. It's just…" He glanced down at the ground and back up at me, his eyes beaming. "The possibility of going back out there and feeling the rush of the thing I've invested my entire life to excited me."

Rocking beside him, a part of me felt for him. I wanted him to be happy and do what he loves. I'd never want him to be miserable. His gaze followed the horizon, his jaw tight. This decision wasn't easy for him.

"I want you to be happy, Korbin. I really do. I just wish the one thing that made you happy didn't have the potential to kill you."

The feeling of helplessness and hopelessness the night of the accident crippled me. I never wanted to experience that again. Not knowing if he was going to live or die or if he'd ever make a full recovery even if he did live was terrifying.

He blinked at me with a concerning gaze. "Bull riding isn't the only thing that makes me happy." He shook his head knowingly. "I know a part of me will miss it. But I need you and Kadence in my life more than I need the rodeo and that leaderboard." He relaxed against the back of his chair as we rocked and watched the sun rise. "I'm gonna be okay." He sighed. "We all are."

"I know we will." I squeezed his hand tightly. "I don't wanna lose you."

He squeezed mine back. "I don't wanna lose you, either."

I knew the upcoming months, and even years, weren't going to be easy, but I believed we could work through whatever was thrown at us.

KORBIN

The next day, Kailyn hadn't been feeling well, but she insisted on coming with Kadence and me to a nearby park anyway. Her skin was pale, and dark circles lined her eyes. I told her she should've stayed home. She sat on a bench nearby as I pushed Kadence on the swings.

"Higher, Daddy! Hiiigher!" Kadence squealed.

"Hold on tight." I laughed and pushed her higher.

Looking over at Kailyn, she smiled, but something didn't feel right. She was looking worse by the minute, and I knew we needed to get her back home and straight to bed.

"Kadence. Kailyn's not feeling well, so we're going to be

leaving soon, okay?" I said, glancing at Kailyn again.

Kadence jumped off the swing, midair, landing on the mulch below. "It's okay. We can go now." She grabbed my hand, and we started over to where Kailyn was.

Kailyn stood from the bench and reached out toward Kadence. Then suddenly, her smile faded, and she collapsed onto the ground.

I sucked in a sharp breath. "Kailyn!" I rushed toward her.

Dropping to my knees, I scooped her up into my arms. "Somebody help!" I shouted at the nearly empty park.

Glancing around, a woman stood nearby with her kids, wide eyed.

"Call nine-one-one!" I choked out. "Kailyn, honey. Come on. Wake up. What happened? What's wrong?" I checked for a pulse and breathed a sigh of relief as I felt the thump against my fingertips.

"Kailyn!" Kadence screamed from behind me. "What's wrong with her, Daddy?"

I turned to Kadence. She was terrified and was holding Kailyn's phone in her hand. She looked up at the sky and cried, "Mommy. Please don't take Kailyn from me, too. Please let her be okay."

Moments later, sirens blared in the distance. A woman ran over to the fence to flag down the EMTs as they pulled up.

Two men jumped out of the ambulance and opened the back door. One pulled a stretcher out while the other grabbed a medical bag and rushed over to Kailyn.

"What happened?" The gray-haired, older gentleman checked her pulse.

I shook my head. "I don't know. She said she wasn't

feeling well earlier, and as we were leaving, she just collapsed."

They placed her onto the stretcher and wheeled her over to the ambulance. "Does she have a medical history?"

"Yeah," I blurted. "She had a heart transplant a little over a year ago." I pointed to her scar.

My mind was a blur. So much was going on around me, but I couldn't move. I just watched helplessly as flashes of Veronica the night of the accident tore through my mind, ripping every fiber of my being to shreds. I'd already lost one woman I loved. I couldn't go through that pain again.

Finally, I found the strength to move and stepped closer to the ambulance. One of the EMTs stopped me. "Sir, you can't come with us. Not with the child." He glanced down at Kadence.

I nodded because I couldn't find any words. She had to be okay. Had to be.

The entire drive to the hospital, I was in a daze. Kadence sobbed in her booster seat behind me. "It's okay, Kadie Bug." I handed my phone to her. "Can you call Nana and have her pick you up at the hospital, please?"

Looking back at her through the rear-view mirror, I clenched my jaw and gripped the steering wheel tightly. I hated seeing her so upset.

When we arrived, my mom was standing by the emergency entrance.

She rushed up to me. "What's wrong with Kailyn?"

"I don't know yet," I said in a hurry. "I'll call you as soon as I know something. I need to get in there," I said, glancing inside through the glass doors. "Can you take Kadence, please?"

Kadence tugged on my shirt. "But, Daddy. I wanna stay with you." Her bottom lip quivered and she wiped her eyes.

Bending down, I grabbed her arms gently. "I know you do, but I need to figure out what's going on with Kailyn first. They won't let kids go back there just yet, but as soon as they do, I'll tell Nana to bring you back. Okay?"

She nodded. "She's gonna be okay. Right, Daddy?"

I kissed the top of her head and wrapped her in a hug. "I sure hope so, kiddo."

After they drove away, I headed inside. I'd only hoped I was prepared, no matter what happened.

Stepping up to the front desk, I was greeted by a woman I knew from high school. I couldn't remember her name, so I glanced down at her nametag. *Pamela.* She looked pretty much the same except shorter hair and no braces.

"Hey, Korbin. How can I help you?" She smiled.

"My girlfriend was just brought in by ambulance," I said, suddenly aware I'd admitted to someone else that Kailyn was my girlfriend even though I hated labels. "Kailyn North."

She typed her name into the computer as I nervously tapped my fingers on the counter.

"Okay." She wrote my name on a sticker and handed it to me. "Put this on the left side of your shirt and go to the large, wooden door around the corner. One of the nurses will meet you there and lead you back to her room."

"Okay, thank you." I slapped the sticker on and rushed around the corner.

The door opened and the nurse guided me down the

hallway. "Follow me, please." She looked over her shoulder as we walked. "Is there anyone else you need us to call for her?"

Her words reminded me of the fact I hadn't heard her talk a lot about her family, and the only friend I knew of she had in Montana was Leesa.

"No, thank you." I pulled Kailyn's phone out of my pocket. "I can do it."

Scrolling through her contacts, I found her mom's number and called to tell her what had happened. It went straight to voicemail. *Great.* Then I sent a text to Leesa letting her know.

"Here we are." The nurse opened the door to her room.

Kailyn was asleep on the bed in the small hospital room. She was hooked up to monitors, and my heart ached seeing her like that. I wanted to trade places with her. I recalled how not too long ago she'd been sitting by my bedside.

I neared the bed. "We have to stop meeting like this," I joked, even though she probably wouldn't hear me.

My chest burned as I fought the emotion bubbling up inside of me. Humor probably wasn't appropriate but it was all I had to keep me from losing my mind at the moment.

Grabbing her hand, I squeezed softly. "If this is my payback for the torment I put you through while I was in my coma…you win."

Glancing up at the monitor, I watched each wave of her heartbeat dance across the screen. Veronica's heart beating in her chest. Keeping her alive.

It had only been minutes, but it seemed like hours had passed as I sat there, waiting for the doctor to come in. I typed in a text to Max to see if he was working.

Me: Are you working right now? At hospital with

Kailyn. Room D-4. No updates from doctor.

Him: Yeah. Be down in a second.

A few minutes later, there was a knock on the door, and Max walked in.

I stood in a hurry. "Max, what's going on, man?" I glanced at my watch. "I haven't even talked to a doctor, yet." I gulped. "Is it her heart?"

"Okay, calm down." He raised his hands. "I already read her chart and talked to Dr. Stryker who triaged her. This is very common in patients after transplants. Her immune system is still very weak, and the immunosuppressants she's been taking make it hard for her body to fight off infections," he explained. "It could take up to a couple of years for her body to be back to normal."

I fell back into the chair. "So she's gonna be okay, then?" I sighed.

"Yes." He nodded once, firmly. "She should be just fine with some rest and an aggressive round of antibiotics. We're going to run a few more tests and keep her overnight for observation, but other than that, she should be okay to go home tomorrow."

I jumped up and hugged him. "Thank you, Max." I sighed. "I thought I had lost her, too."

He raised an eyebrow. "You're really in love with her, aren't you?"

"Yes." I glanced at her and back to him. "I know it sounds crazy, but I am."

He pulled me into another half hug and slapped me on the back. "It's not crazy. Remember Daniel?" I nodded. "Well, he married his wife after a month of dating, and they just celebrated their eleventh wedding anniversary." He smiled. "I'm happy for you, man." He walked toward the door. "I have to get back to my patients now. I'm glad she's going to be okay. Dr. Stryker said he'd be in shortly."

"Okay, thanks again." I threw a hand up at him.

He laughed. "Just doing my job. Calming your ass down, as usual."

I chuckled, and after he left the room, I quickly called Kadence to tell her the good news.

Kailyn groaned. Her eyes blinked open, and she groggily looked around the room.

I squeezed her hand. "Kailyn? I'm here," I reassured her. "Are you feeling okay? Do you need anything? Does anything hurt?"

"You sure do ask a lot of questions." She winced as she tried to roll over. "And, yes, we really do have to stop meeting like this."

"You heard me?" I laughed.

"Yes." Her tone grew serious. "Everything."

Tears pooled beneath her lashes. She blinked, and they ran down the side of her face, landing on her pillow.

"Why are you crying?" I grabbed her hand. "Are you hurting?"

She shook her head. "No. I'm just glad I'm okay, and that you're here."

I swallowed hard. "Seeing you collapse in front of me like that scared the hell out of me. I thought I lost you." I sat on the edge of the bed beside her. "I held my breath as they loaded you into that ambulance and wondered what I'd find when I arrived here at the hospital." She blinked up at me. "When they pulled away with you, part of my heart went with you. I love you so much," I said, placing a kiss on her lips.

She smiled. "I love you, too. I hate to tell you this." She frowned. "But you're stuck with me for a while." She paused for a moment then grinned. "Hopefully forever."

Forever. I liked the sound of that. The first time I thought I'd found love forever, though, it was taken from me way too soon. Only, this time, I had to believe *forever* would be us growing old together, having more children, and one day, even watching our grandchildren play on the farm. A future with Kailyn was exactly what I wanted.

Chapter Twenty-Four

Kailyn

FTER A GOOD NIGHT'S sleep, I felt much better. Blinking my eyes open, I turned to find Leesa staring at me, making me jump.

"Are you trying to give me a heart attack?" I groaned. "Have you been watching me sleep? Creep."

She laughed. "Someone has to babysit you while Korbin's gone."

"Where'd he go?" I glanced around the room.

"There was an issue with one of the tractors back at the ranch, and he had to go take care of it." She quickly held up a hand. "Don't worry. It's nothing major. He told me he'd be back shortly and encouraged me to stay with you until he got back."

I laughed. "Of course he did."

She grew quiet and frowned. "I have to tell you something." She paced the floor.

I sat up in bed and leaned toward her. "What's wrong? What is it?"

She shook her hands nervously. "I knew Korbin's wife was the one who died in the accident that night."

Before I could respond, she bolted to the side of the bed and grabbed my hand. "But you made me promise, swear even, that I wouldn't tell you details about that night, even if you begged me to." She sat on the edge of the bed, her gaze full of regret. "I'm sorry. I should've told you before you started working for him."

Grabbing her hand, I processed what she'd just said. "So that's the reason you and Jake were acting strange at breakfast when I told you I was going to apply." I shrugged. "It's okay. You were only doing what I'd asked you to do. Honestly, I'm glad you didn't tell me because, if you had, I wouldn't be as happy and in love as I am right now." Leaning forward, I hugged her.

"I'm so glad you're not mad at me." Tears formed beneath her lashes. "Damn hormones," she said, making us both laugh.

There was a knock on the door.

"Come in." Leesa moved to the chair by the bed.

It was Max. "How're you feeling this morning?"

He was the doctor on the floor they admitted me to after leaving the ER last night. I was convinced Korbin had planned it that way on purpose. Apparently, Korbin trusted his best friend more than the other doctors.

He moved around the room, taking notes and checking the monitor.

I smiled. "Honestly, I feel like a new person. I have so much energy I could probably run laps around the hospital."

He laughed. "Let's focus on walking for now. You can run laps later." He opened my chart and scanned it for a moment. "All of your tests came back normal. As long as you feel okay, you're good to go."

Looking down at my hands, I fidgeted with the blanket. I was still a little nervous about leaving the hospital, and Max must have noticed.

"Hey." He patted my shoulder. "This is not uncommon of heart transplant patients. Your body is still a little weaker than normal, and it's hard to fight off infections. It's just a virus. You'll be just fine." His gaze was comforting. "Now, go home and enjoy spending time with Korbin because he's driving me crazy. If you don't go home to him soon, I may be running laps around the hospital myself," he joked.

I immediately called Korbin to tell him the good news.

Korbin hurried into the room looking like he'd just ran a marathon. "Let's get you home." He stepped outside the room and came back in with a wheelchair.

I rolled my eyes. "Korbin, I don't need a wheelchair. I'm perfectly capable of walking out of here. I feel fine. Really." After a night of sleep and an antibiotic, I really did feel great.

He motioned for me to get into the wheelchair anyway. I looked to Leesa for help, and she shrugged.

"Thanks a lot. You're really no help."

She raised her hands then pointed between me and Korbin. "Hey, I'm not getting involved with that." She gave me a quick hug. "I'll call you later to see how you're doing.

Let me know if you need anything." She smiled.

"Thank you." Korbin moved to the side so Leesa could exit.

"No problem, but you must know." She cut her eyes at me. "She called me a creep for watching her sleep. That's some kind of b-f-f abuse, I'm sure."

He chuckled.

I smirked and motioned for her to leave. "Are you my b-f-f or his?"

She laughed. "Glad to see you're going to be okay. I'll talk to you later."

Korbin glanced at me and back to the wheelchair. I knew there was no winning with him. "Let's go. You don't wanna overdo it right now."

Sighing in defeat, I got into the wheelchair, and he wheeled me outside to his truck that was parked by the curb.

"Where's Kadence?"

He opened the door so I could get in.

"She's at home waiting for you."

"Alone?" I winced as I stepped up into the truck. My ribs were still sore from where I collapsed.

"Not exactly..." He quickly closed the door before I could respond and rushed around to his side.

Gazing out the window, I took a deep breath and thought about how lucky I was to be alive.

We turned onto the dirt drive and started toward the ranch. There were welcome home posters and balloons all over the fence posts leading up to the house and they made me smile. *Kadence.*

Korbin grabbed my hand and squeezed. "I'm so glad you're okay." He kissed the back of my hand. "I love you."

I smiled. "I love you, too." My eyes widened as we neared the house. "Korbin…"

He chuckled. "Don't be mad." He shrugged. "It was Kadence's idea. She planned and decorated by herself." I scowled at him, and his eyes widened. "Honestly."

He parked the truck and came around to open my door. As soon as I stepped out about twenty people yelled, "Welcome home!" in unison. Some of them I recognized, and some I didn't.

Kadence ran up and hugged me tightly. "Surprise, Kailyn! Welcome home!" She giggled. "I planned this all by myself. Do you love your surprise?" She bounced up and down.

Bending down, I kissed her forehead. "I love it so much. Thank you."

Making my way toward everyone, I was greeted with hugs. Jamie, the girl from the diner was there. Leesa and Jake were there. *I can't believe Leesa hid this from me. That little sneak.* Zach and some of the other farm hands were there. Ella and William were there, also, along with a few of Korbin's friends I didn't know.

I took turns saying hello and thanking them for the well wishes. After about an hour of visiting I was starting to feel tired.

Korbin wasn't kidding when he said everyone knows everyone in this town. I'd have to catch up and learn who everyone was.

"Okay," Korbin said, as if right on cue. "Thank you for

coming, but Kailyn needs to get some rest now." He cut his eyes at me knowingly.

We all said our goodbyes, and Korbin, Kadence, and I went inside.

KORBIN

Kailyn ambled upstairs to take a shower and get comfortable. Walking outside, I found Kadence sitting on the bank by the creek, throwing sticks into the water.

I sat down beside her. "Are you okay, Kadie Bug?"

She ignored me and threw another stick into the water.

"Kadence? What's wrong?"

She inhaled a sharp breath and looked at me with tear-filled eyes. "I don't want anything to happen to you or Kailyn." She looked back at the creek and threw a small rock into the water with a plop.

I grabbed her hand and pulled her onto my lap. "Hey. Look at me."

"I know you're scared. You've been through a lot more than most little girls your age." I paused to gather my thoughts. "None of us know what tomorrow brings, honey. I'm not going to lie to you." Her chin trembled. "All we can do is love each person who is a part of our lives and enjoy every moment we have with them." I wiped the tears from her cheeks and pulled her into a hug. "I'm so proud of you, Kadence. I love you so much, and I promise you I'm going to do everything in my power to keep Kailyn in our lives."

She pulled back and blinked up at me through small tears. "I think you should marry her."

I almost choked on air when she said that. *You should marry her.* The words echoed through my mind. It was so soon. Was I ready?

Kadence turned and continued throwing rocks.

Glancing out over the water, I thought about it. Veronica and I were high school sweethearts, so we dated for years before we got married. Was I willing to ask Kailyn to marry me so soon? I loved her. That much I knew for sure. Were we moving too fast? Or did it really matter how long we'd known each other if both of our hearts were in the same place, and willing to take that leap? I picked a rock up and threw it into the water as I pondered the idea. After all, I knew plenty of couples personally who'd only dated for a few weeks or a few months before getting hitched, and they're still going strong years later.

Can anyone really put a time limit on love?

"Daddy? Are you okay?" Kadence touched my arm. "I'm sorry if I upset you." She frowned.

"No, no, no, sweetheart. You didn't upset me. It's not that," I reassured her. "You just caught me by surprise. That's all." I smiled and rubbed her hand. "It's just that…I think maybe it's a little too soon."

"Do you love her?" She tilted her head to the side. "Because I do. A lot." She wiped her nose with her arm. "Mommy said if you love someone you never let them go."

I sighed, rubbing her hair. "You know…you're wise beyond your years, kiddo. How did I ever get so lucky to have you as a daughter?"

She giggled. "I am awesome."

I kissed the top of her head. "Your mom would be so proud of you."

She sighed. "I hope so. I want to be as perfect as she was when I grow up."

I smiled. "Oh, you already are, Kadie Bug. You already are."

She cuddled up to me as the sun disappeared behind the trees. Kadence had to grow up so quickly after her mom died. It broke my heart, but she was so strong and quite mature to be so young.

Maybe Kadence was right. I couldn't ignore the instant connection I'd had with Kailyn, and we'd already been through so much together in such a short time. There was no guarantee of a tomorrow, let alone a next year.

Life is too short to wait for what I already know in my heart I want.

"Hey." I smiled at her. "I think you're right. I'm going to ask Kailyn to marry me. There's one problem, though…"

Her eyes narrowed. "What?"

"I have no clue how to do it." I frowned. "If only I knew someone who was really good at planning things…" I sighed.

She perked up. "Me, Daddy! Let me help."

"Okay, I guess," I said, hiding a laugh. "You have to keep it our secret though, okay?" I narrowed my eyes at her playfully. "No giving it away."

She made a zipping motion across her lips. "My lips are sealed."

We both laughed. "Okay. Now, let's go in and eat dinner. I'm starving."

Chapter Twenty-Five

Kailyn

One Month Later

THE FALL RUSH OF harvesting and distributing crops
had ended, and I was thankful for some time off from
crunching numbers and calculating the ranch's bottom line. I rocked back and forth on the front porch, enjoying the crisp autumn air. Closing my eyes, I pulled my plush
blanket up under my chin and inhaled deeply. I opened my
eyes and peered out over the peaceful ranch, thankful my
body continued to grow stronger each day. It was hard getting used to the fact that my immune system just wasn't as
strong as it used to be before my transplant.

Kadence bounced out of the house in what looked like
ten layers of clothing and multiple toboggans on her head.
"Are you ready to go on our horseback ride to our favorite
overlook?" she beamed. "We have to hurry. It may snow

soon."

I laughed. "How do you even move under all of that?"

She moved like a robot as she struggled to lift her arms above her head. "Like this."

Standing up, I scanned the property. "Don't you wanna wait on your dad?" I asked, glancing out at the barn.

Where is he anyway?

She opened the door, motioning for me to go inside. "No, he already left." She shrugged. "He said he'd meet us up there."

I narrowed my eyes at her. She seemed to be up to something. Why was she so excited about a horseback ride in the freezing cold?

She stuck her bottom lip out and batted her long eyelashes.

I gave in and walked inside to humor her. "Okay, fine. Let's go."

She squealed and followed behind me.

After dressing warmly and bundling up for the ride, we headed out to the barn. The horses were already saddled and ready to go.

"Did you...?" I started, turning to Kadence.

She snickered and shrugged. "Get on. Let's go."

I shook my head, dismissing how strange the evening was becoming, and mounted Snowflake. Kadence took off in a hurry, leaving me behind. "Come on, Kailyn. Keep up!"

KORBIN

Looking down at my watch, I realized it was almost time for

Kadence and Kailyn to arrive. My throat felt like sandpaper as I tried to swallow. It was dusk and cold outside, yet I was sweating and my nerves were on edge. My hands trembled as I pulled the small, black box out of my pocket. I opened it to check that it was still in there and paced back and forth, waiting for them to arrive. Taking my cowboy hat off, I exhaled and ran a hand through my hair, before placing it back on my head. Many thoughts raced through my mind as I waited.

What if she says no? What if it doesn't work out? What if I freeze up, and I'm not able to ask her? What if I don't ask her and spend the rest of my life wondering what if? Am I doing the right thing?

The *"what ifs"* would have to wait, for now. The only one I cared about was the, *"what if I don't ask her to marry me and regret it later"?*

In the distance leaves crunched and sticks popped.

They're almost here.

The cold front had moved in, and I could see my breath as I exhaled. Taking another deep breath, I reminded myself of one thing...*Life's too short to wait.*

Kailyn

As we neared the end of the trail, there were red rose petals scattered on the ground leading to the field.

"What's this?" I asked, turning to Kadence. "What's going on?"

She smiled and rode off ahead of me, leaving me behind again. My heart raced, and my breath caught as I continued through the clearing into the field.

Korbin was standing under a large oak tree, and I smiled at how handsome he was. He looked delicious in his button-up polo and khakis with his nice coat and scarf. Even though he was dressed out of his norm, he was still wearing his cowboy hat that I loved so much. I trotted over to him. Twinkling solar lights lit up the tree. They looked magical.

He helped me down from Snowflake, looking nervous. His hands trembled. "You look so beautiful."

My cheeks warmed at his compliment. "What's going on?" I swallowed with anticipation while I waited for him to say something.

He inhaled slowly. "I love you, and if there's anything I've learned over the past few months, it's that life is unexpected." He exhaled nervously. "We never know one day from the next what's going to happen." He squeezed my hands in his. "I need you in my life more than I need air to breathe."

He wiped the tears from my cheeks.

"You've helped me heal, and every day I'm with you, I want to be a better man." He kissed my hand. "In such a short amount of time, you've shown me what it feels like to love again, and I want to keep this feeling for forever."

He extended a hand, motioning toward the tree.

I took a step toward the tree to read the carving in the wood. It was a heart, and in the middle was: **Korbin + Kailyn + Kadence = Family.**

Eyes wide, I turned to find Korbin on one knee with a round diamond engagement ring sparkling in a small velvet box. The diamond was set with many smaller stones, lining the white gold band. It was breathtaking and perfect.

He looked up at me and smiled—his bright smile

reaching all the way up to his eyes. "Kailyn North. Will you marry me?"

Kadence rushed by his side, holding a large decorated chalkboard that read: **Will you please be my stepmom?**

I covered my mouth, gathering myself enough to nod and say, "Yes." My heart swelled as I looked down into their eyes.

Korbin and Kadence looked at each other. "She said yes?" he asked, like he almost didn't believe it himself.

She clapped her hands together. "Yep! I told you she would."

His hands trembled as he slid the ring onto my finger.

Looking up, I blinked as powdery snowflakes landed on my lashes.

"It's snowing!" Kadence yelled, running around, catching snowflakes on her tongue.

Standing up in front of me, Korbin took my face in his hands and kissed me, taking my breath away.

Breaking the kiss, he turned to Kadence and held out his hands. "She said yes!"

"And it's snowing!" she added.

He laughed. "Yes, and it's snowing." Then picked her up and spun her around.

I giggled as I watched them run around in the snow. This was going to be my life now. *Forever.*

Turning back to the tree, I traced the heart with my fingers, finding it hard to believe the decisions I'd made on my journey to self-discovery had led me here. I was the city girl who fell in love with the country boy, and my heart was happy for that. After all of the things we'd been through, we were finally going to have our happily ever after. Our love story may have been sudden and unforeseen, but I welcomed the unexpected moments in life because, so far, this one has been the best yet.

The End

Contact Information

Thank you for reading, "Hart of Country," by Kris Nacole. If you enjoyed this novel, you may also enjoy Kris' debut novel, "Love Him Back". Please see website below for more details.

Learn more about Kris Nacole and her books at: www.krisnacole.com or follow her at:

Facebook: www.facebook.com/authorkrisnacole.

Twitter: www.twitter.com/krisnacole15

Instagram: AuthorKrisNacole

Snap Chat: KrisNacole

If this book had a playlist:

Cole Swindell – *You Should Be Here*
Luke Bryan – *Strip it Down*
Luke Bryan – *Do I*
Rascal Flatts – *I Melt*
Rascal Flatts – *What Hurts the Most*
John Legend – *All of Me*
Keith Anderson – *Every Time I Hear Your Name*
Labrinth – *Beneath your Beautiful*
Miranda Lambert – *Over You*
Blake Shelton – *Who Are You When I'm Not Looking*
Lonestar – *Amazed*
Lonestar – *I'm Already There*
Casting Crowns – *Just be Held*
Chris Young – *Who I Am With You*
Chris Young – *The Man I Want to Be*
Disturbed – *The Sound of Silence*
Staind – *Epiphany*
Staind – *It's been a While*
Candlebox – *Far Behind*
Blake McGrath – *Earned it (cover)*
Fever Ray – *The Wolf*
Tobi and Jona Selle – *Love Me Like You Do (Cover)*
Florida Georgia Line – *Anything Goes*
Ryan Bingham – *Broken Heart Tattoos*
Tracy Lawrence – *Paint me a Birmingham*
Tracy Lawrence – *Alibis*
Us and Our Daughters – *Lost and Found*
Trace Adkins – *Every Light in the House is On*

Somo – The Weekend – *The Trilogy (Medley)*
Jason Mraz – *I Won't Give Up*
Tim McGraw and Faith Hill – *It's Your Love*
Gavin Rossdale – *Love Remains the Same*
Dierks Bentley – *I Wanna Make You Close Your Eyes*
Saving Abel – *Addicted*
Saving Abel – *The Sex is Good*
Brad Paisley & Alison Krauss – *Whiskey Lullaby*
Dove Cameron – *If Only*
SoMo – Calvin Harris/Disciples – *How Deep is Your Love (Rendition)*
Sia – *Elastic Heart*
Billy Currington – *Let me Down Easy*
Kane Brown – *Used to Love you Sober*
Kane Brown – *Forgetting is the Hardest Part*
Lana Del Rey – *Gods and Monsters*
Lena Fayre – *This World*
Selena Gomez – *Good For You*
Miley Cyrus – *Adore You*
Miley Cyrus – *The Climb*
Miley Cyrus – *When I Look at You*
William Michael Morgan – *I met a girl*
Brad Paisley – *Today*
Christina Perri – *Human*

Acknowledgments

To my loving **children:** Thank you for continuing to encourage mommy to follow her dreams. I've always told you both to follow your dreams, no matter what anyone says, and you always remind me that I need to do the same. I hope I continue to make you proud and be the best mom I can possibly be. I'm so proud of both of you, and I hope I'm proving to you that you can do anything you set your mind to. Mommy loves you both to Heaven and back.

To my loving and supportive **family:** Thank you for always believing in me and encouraging me to follow my dreams no matter what roadblocks I may encounter along the way. I love you all so much and couldn't do any of this without you in my corner.

To my **betas:** I can't even begin to thank you enough for your suggestions, criticisms, and support for *Hart of Country.* You have all truly helped open my eyes as a writer and an author, and I thank you for that.

To my fellow **writers:** Thank you for the support you've shown and encouragement you've given me along this journey so far. Thank you for being *my people* I can rely on and reach out to when I need a reminder that writing isn't easy, and we all have moments of doubt.

To my editor, **Megan:** Thank you so much for helping me not only make *Hart of Country* the best it can be, but for also helping me grow as a writer. After your feedback for *Love Him Back*, I feel I really did grow as a writer and that it really shows in this book. You've helped open my eyes and mind to show me I do have what it takes to be a great writer. You're amazing and I can't thank you enough for all the time you've spent on making *Hart of Country* great!

To my **Silent Branch girls:** Thank you all for continuing to be so supportive of me through my writing journey. You've encouraged and supported me in so many ways. Most of you have been in my life for many years. I know I always have you ladies to fall back on when I need someone to catch me at my weakest points. You're more like sisters to me than friends. I love you girls so much. Thank you again for always having my back.

To my **Street Team—Kris' Kisses:** I don't even know where to start with y'all. You hold such a special place in my heart. You're my street team—the one group of people who constantly have my back and continue to tell the world about me and my books. I couldn't do this without you. Thank you for loving me and being such amazing supporters. Also, thank you for never judging me or my decisions. You all ROCK, and I love you hard!

To the best friends a girl could ever have, **Jess, Heather, Amy, Ashley, Jodi and Margo:** Y'all have been there for me from the beginning. (Some of you since we were five years old.) You'll never know how much I value your friendship and how much I love you girls. You've all been there for me through the good, the bad, and the ugly. You've never once judged me, and you've always loved me, no matter my faults. I'm so blessed to have amazing, strong, beautiful, and supportive best friends by my side. Thank you for sharing this journey with me. Love you, ladies!

To all the **authors** who have given me guidance throughout this journey: Thank you from the bottom of my heart for taking the time to help guide me along this journey. Your advice has helped me become a better writer, and I thank you for that. Some of you even welcomed me with open arms into your personal lives and have become like family to me.

To my dear friend **Lisa**: There aren't enough words to thank you for everything you've done to help me through this. I'm so thankful for you and wish I could somehow repay you for the hell I've put you through at times over the past couple of years. You're not just a friend, you're family. Love you, girl. Thank you.

Last, but certainly not least...to **my readers**: Thank you, from the bottom of my heart, for taking the time to read *Hart of Country*. I hope you're as touched by reading Korbin and Kailyn's love story as I was writing it. Without your support, I wouldn't be able to follow my dreams, so thank you again. You all mean the world to me.

"As long as you keep reading, I promise to keep writing." – Kris Nacole